OUT OF THE SHADOWS

SOUL RESTORATION THROUGH THE POWER OF CHOICE

CARMEN ESTHER SANDOVAL

Published by:
Upward Focus Productions
28251 Paseo El Siena
Laguna Niguel, California 92677

ISBN-978-0-9980444-1-5

Printed in the United States of America

Cover Art "Cocoon" by Carmen Esther Sandoval

Please note that the publisher has elected to capitalize certain pronouns that refer to the Father, Son and Holy Spirit, as a form of respect, despite the fact that this may violate grammatical rules.

DEDICATION

For all those challenged by emotional wounds and demonic oppression, pressing through for healing and freedom is not only an act of faith, it is also an act of courage.

This book is dedicated to those who exercise courage by choosing to seek the restorative power of God through Jesus Christ. May God's healing and deliverance power be demonstrated in and through your life and may you be used of God to help others find freedom in Christ Jesus by the power of the Holy Spirit.

ACKNOWLEDGMENTS

Out of the Shadows could not have been possible without the encouragement and support of my Heavenly Father, Jesus and Holy Spirit who have guided me every step of the way.

My deepest appreciation to Pastor Mario Procopio for his prophetic words which sparked the vision for this project before a word had ever been written.

Also, special thanks to Pastor's Terry and Debbie Hilgen and Pastor Rukins McKinley for their encouragement and prayers.

Sincere gratitude to Kathryn Smith Fogarty, Sharon Hatok, Carol Kraft, Audrey Morgan, Sandy Mullen and Jeanette Shattuck for their prayers on my behalf and on behalf of this project.

Special thanks to Copy Editor, Audrey Morgan and Graphic Designer, Walter Baker.

FORWARD

"I am pleased to recommend Carmen Sandoval's excellent book, especially to anyone who has felt hopeless, languished in guilt and shame, believed lies, or has suffered depression. This is a book about freedom and the journey to a new life."

Jay Grant, Pastor
Little Church by the Sea
Laguna Beach, California

"Life is a journey that creates layers of memories. As you peel away each layer, you recognize that you made a choice to forgive and be free of the memory or you decided to hold on to the burden that keeps weighing you down. This book will guide you through each step to wholeness as it uncovers each layer through the stories and examples. May this be your journey to freedom and peace."

Dr. Ana Aguayo-Bryant

TABLE OF CONTENTS

Part B

Allegory of the Mouse

Part C

Allegory of the Sheep

INTRODUCTION

Distortion of self-image has wreaked havoc in the lives of many men and women, stealing precious years and killing countless relationships. I was one of those casualties of a warped mirror. Because of my personal brokenness I believed lies about myself and about my future. Those lies brought me to the brink of self-destruction in a suicide attempt.

Late one December evening I yielded to hopelessness and decided to drive my car off a cliff toward an oil dike. As I started the decent, I remembered being taught as a child that there was a heaven and a hell. In that moment I cried out from the depths of my heart to a God I was not sure existed. My exact prayer was "God, I don't know if you are real, but if you are please help me. I don't want to go to hell but what I am living with is hell on earth." In an instant I came out of my depressed stupor and slowly applied the break and then backed my car off the cliff. In His great mercy God had heard my cry and rescued me. I sat in silence for nearly an hour as I contemplated what I had almost done and realized that God had helped me and made Himself real to me.

I had never watched Christian programming but a week later as I flipped channels, I heard Pastor Chuck Smith Senior of Calvary Chapel, Costa Mesa talking about the love of God. He explained how God demonstrated that love toward us by sending Jesus to die in our place. Growing up I had heard a lot about the fire and brimstone of God but little about the love of God. At that moment I imagined Jesus crashing into the oil dike, blowing up in flames and going to hell in my place. I suddenly understood what the cross was about and I asked Jesus to forgive me. I gave Him my life and asked Him to help me experience the Father's love.

As to the hell I was living with on earth, it has been the work of the Holy Spirit over these many years to bring light to the dark chambers of my soul and heal my brokenness. He has renewed my mind and restored me to relationship with a loving Heavenly Father. I was poured out like a glass of spilled wine as my flaws were exposed by the winepress of life. But by the grace of God I have found my identity, and hope has been renewed.

The following stories are about my journey through restoration of the soul and those of others I have met along the way. Satan, who is the thief, tried to steal, kill, and destroy my life, but Jesus came so that I could regain my true identity and have the abundant life He promised me in John 10:10.

Are you the person God created you to be or have others convinced you of a lie? Have circumstances beyond your control dictated your value and robbed you of your inheritance before you ever had an opportunity to claim it? As you read these pages, I invite you to investigate what you believe to be true about yourself and to be brutally honest about how you came to that assessment. Unwrapped and vulnerable I bring to you accounts of myself and others who have taken this journey. My intent is to demonstrate to you the very real power of God to deliver each of us from the power of the lies and traps set for our destruction and the very real power of the Holy Spirit to restore the human soul.

I invite you to look into the mirror of your soul and should you see a distorted reflection there know that you are never left without recourse. For every marred image the loving Heavenly Father has provided a means of restoration to the beautiful person He initially created you to be. We each were formed in the image of our Creator. Anything that does not reflect His image is a work of deception and distortion. It is the power of the Holy Spirit that will strip away the facades and begin the detailed and meticulous work of restoration. Our part is to yield to the Holy Spirit and to align ourselves with truth. It is the truth we know that will set us free.

Sorrow of heart, loss of hope, destruction of the mind is what I see on every side. Many lives are like a war zone or a city ruined by a great storm. Their walls have been shattered and their gates have been burned with fire. Through His great grace walls can be built up and gates restored that they no longer be a reproach. He will strengthen us for the good work that He wants done. By His grace and strength, we will prosper and we will rebuild.

We will discuss what restoration is, the power of choice to allow that process to flourish and how we can walk in our true identity. Before you read further ask the Holy Spirit to help you see yourself as you really are and just as importantly, ask Him to help you see who you are not so that you too can have the thief arrested and your true identity restored.

PART A

ALLEGORY OF
THE BIRD

CHAPTER 1

BEAUTIFUL MELODY

The cave was dark and damp. Too weak to move, she curled up in a corner wishing she had never opened her eyes to see this day. If she could just sleep it would numb the pain. But how could she sleep when her heart was pounding with fear? She sank deeper into the darkness of the cave and hoped no one would find her before she was strong enough to escape.

It had all happened so quickly and come out of nowhere. For a moment she was paralyzed and then she felt the surge of warm blood oozing from the wound. The large black crow had swooped down and bitten her left side taking a chunk of flesh. As blood gushed from her side she dashed for the cave before he had a chance to come at her again. Anxiously she waited for her throbbing body to recover from the shock and trauma. When daylight broke, she slowly inched toward a grassy spot and drank in the comfort of the morning dew.

The little bird, with big eyes and silken feathers, had always been smaller than the other feathered creatures. Despite her best efforts, when she opened her mouth to sing all she could do was coo. The mocking and the crowded nest soon forced her to make her own way in the forest.

Now she hid herself from the other birds for fear of being ridiculed. They had taunted her because she was small, then because she could not sing, and now she had this ugly wound in her side. The little bird decided that something was terribly wrong with her for this to have happened. Shame flooded over her as she saw her reflection in a puddle of water.

Day after day she stayed low and kept to herself as she waited for her feathers to grow back and cover her wound. As strength returned, she made her way up toward the rocky places beyond the trees, leaving her family behind. She reasoned that the lizards and the spiders that lived among the rocks could neither sing nor fly. They would not make fun of her. She hoped that the crow would not go to the trouble of looking for her in the rocky places.

By day she ate berries, pretending to be content, but by night she cried herself to sleep. There was less danger among the rocks but she was lonely and even her cooing had been silenced by her heavy heart. The very rocks that protected her from the crow also barred her from the forest she so loved.

One evening, a nightingale heard her faint crying. She followed the sound and gently flew down beside the little bird. The lovely melody she sang was soft and soothing. She sang about a healing stream where love flowed deep and wide. Night after night she sang, comforting the little bird. It was only a melody, but each day the little bird looked forward to the nightingale's return. A glimmer of hope had sparked within her grieving heart. After many days, she had the courage to ask the nightingale to lead her to the stream she sang about, the one filled with mercy and loving kindness.

She was stunned by the beauty of the clear water shimmering in the sunlight, surrounded by soft ferns. Slowly she took a sip, and then another, as cool refreshment filled her body and her soul. As she stood on the bank, she was careful not to drink too quickly. Each day she returned, going a little deeper and drinking a little longer. Each night the nightingale sang to her about the One who had created her and the healing waters.

The weariness left her body, and then the sorrow blew away like a leaf in the wind. Finally, the fear was washed away as ripple after ripple of love flowed over her. In time, she realized her wound was gone, taking with it her shame. The time in the cave was a small price to pay for having found this beautiful place of healing and refreshment. The painful memories of the crow became a faded dream. She was so excited that she burst out in a song. It was not like the melody the nightingale sung to her. The little bird with big eyes and silken feathers had a melody of her own. It was bold, strong and loud. It frightened the crows and warned the other birds of trouble.

She was not ashamed to tell about her wounds and her struggle in the cave. But most of all, she shared about the stream of healing waters, and the One who had created it.

Not all the birds listened to her melody or followed her to the stream. But those who did soon filled the forest with songs of hope and joy. The melodies embraced each other as they floated through the air. No longer was she too small, with no song and an ugly wound. She had become more than she ever could have dreamed. Soaring high above the trees, her heart was filled with gratitude to the One who had created her and for the healing stream.

CHAPTER 2

VOICE IN THE MIRROR

Disney Studios released the animated version of *Snow White and the Seven Dwarfs* in 1937. In the original German fairy tale, the Grimm Brothers depict Snow White's stepmother as a woman of great beauty but one filled with pride. Speaking to her image in the mirror she asks who is fairest in the land and in vain satisfaction the mirror replies that she is the fairest in the land. One day the mirror responded that Snow White, at the age of seven, was now more beautiful than the queen. The queen turns green with envy. Her hatred of the child grows daily like a great wild weed. Envy turns to murder as she commands the huntsman to take the child into the forest and kill her. She charges him to bring back the lungs and liver of the child, which she intends to eat. Unable to bring himself to kill the child the huntsman lets her escape into the forest knowing that wild beast will soon devour her.

When the mirror reports that Snow White is still alive and living in the forest with seven dwarfs the queen's anger turns to murderous rage. Disguised as an old peddler, three failed death plots follow until Snow White finally eats of a poisoned apple and falls as dead. The dwarfs weep for her and keep her enshrined in a glass-covered coffin. Miraculously she does not decay although the demon in the mirror reports to the queen that Snow White is now dead. The king's son who is traveling through the forest falls in love with the beauty in the coffin. He begs to have her and as he carries away the coffin, he trips on a tree stump, the poison apple dislodges from her throat and she is resurrected. Consenting to marry the prince they return to the palace. What was the outcome of the wicked queen? She is forced to put on red-hot shoes and dance at the wedding until she drops down dead.

In the United States the 1937 film was listed as a family, musical fantasy animation. In South Africa however, the film receives the equivalent of an "x" rating. Some would even describe it as the first "x" rated animation film. It escaped the Western mind that calling up a demon to speak through a mirror, eating human body parts, sending a child into the forest to be devoured by wild beasts, plots of murder and a queen cursed to dance herself to death were all less then family entertainment. The South Africans recognized violence and witchcraft even when masked with the veneer of animation.

Repeatedly the fairytale reinforces that the mirror never lies and that because of her outward beauty Snow White is both hated and loved. That is part of the fantasy because the voice in the mirror does lie and as it lied to the queen it has lied to many would be queen's generation after generation. The mirror on the wall is not a measure of who is fairest in the land, yet girls the world over grow up fixated on the mirror and what it says to them. The same is true for boys who grow up with a flawed image.

Has the opinion of another defined who you are? Is the voice in the mirror echoing what you heard your parents say? Perhaps it is the voice of your older sister, brother, coach or friends. Or has the voice in the mirror convinced you that you do not measure up to the image in the glossy magazines, the Hollywood divas or the sport stars.

If the voice in the mirror has lied to you it can be silenced. The first step to a recovered identity is a conscious decision on your part to examine the voice and the validity of the words you have accepted about yourself. Did someone convince you that you were unlovely and unlovable, weak and frail, guilty and shameful, stupid or unacceptable? Was there no one to tell you that you were valuable, unique and capable of great things? Were you taught to measure yourself by how you look, by your intellect or by how you perform rather than by the intent of your heart and the strength of your character? "The Lord sees not as man sees, for man looks on the outward appearance, but the Lord look on the heart" (1 Samuel 16:7b).

Outward makeovers, although momentarily gratifying, are but a bandage and will not have lasting results. When the make-up and the fancy clothes are off; when the applause and awards are over you are still left with your thoughts and opinions of yourself. The change has to happen on the inside to be lasting.

The loving Heavenly Father created you and wants you to know how He sees you and how valuable you are to Him. If you allow Him to speak to you, He will silence all the other voices that have spoken ill of you. He is for you and not against you. "For I know the plans I have for you, declares the Lord, plans to prosper you and not to harm you, plans to give you hope and a future" (Jeremiah 29:11).

Identity is a heart issue. The everlasting doors are the doors to your heart. Open the doors to your heart and ask the Lord Jesus to expose every lie that has shaped your self-image. Then ask Him for grace to forgive those through whom those lies were spoken and come out of agreement with them. Give the Holy Spirit permission to shatter the deceptive mirrors you have been looking into. He will start the restoration process as you yield to His work and partnership with Him by daily looking into the clear mirror of the Word of God. It is through the scriptures that He will speak to you as He heals and transforms you into the beautiful person, He created you to be.

"But we all, with open face beholding as in a glass the glory of the Lord, are changed into the same image from glory to glory, even as by the Spirit of the Lord" (2 Corinthians 3:18).

CHAPTER 3

SOUL RESTORATION

In a dream I saw an angel holding a little girl by the hand. She was beautiful but she was crippled. As I took her hand I began to cry because I could not help her. I saw her like a piece of beautiful exotic wood that had been twisted. I looked into her eyes and saw love and grace that reminded me of a delicate flower, but her body was broken. I desperately wanted her straightened out and free to run and play. I woke up weeping.

The core of restoration is the Holy Spirit bringing healing to the soul of man so that he will be in harmony with his Creator. This wholeness is manifested in health, strength and peace of mind. Heavy stones in the heart and splinters of glass in the mind are removed by the Holy Spirit and exchanged for beautiful smooth jewels with which to rebuild the walls of our lives.

"The Spirit of the Lord is upon me, because He has anointed me to preach the gospel to the poor; He has sent Me to heal the brokenhearted. To proclaim liberty to the captives, and recovery of sight to the blind, to set at liberty them that are oppressed; to proclaim the acceptable year of the Lord" (Luke 4:18 and Isaiah 61·1-2). Jesus said this about Himself and He has not changed. The Holy Spirit who is now ministering in the affairs of men on the earth is still performing the work of restoration in all those who will choose to yield to it. By yielding we allow the master surgeon to root out the core of our pain and bring soundness to the places in our lives that are broken, diseased or distressed. He does not bring temporary comfort or partial relief; He brings total healing.

A friend who knows my love for plants brought me a beautiful Lavatera Tree Mallow. The plant had great potential but in the current state was stunted and would soon die because it was root bound. It had been in a large pot for over a year and the roots had no recourse but to wind around each other. The remedy was to pull it out of the pot and with a trowel cut vertical slits along the root ball. Once planted in the ground the roots would extend horizontally bringing it nutriments and stimulating growth. The stunted 4ft plant would then be able to grow into a large tree with its beautiful pink and purple flowers.

Pain causes us to be focused inward. Growth has been stunted and potential locked up inside our souls. But Jesus came to set the captive free. Allowing the Lord to release us from pain, we are then able to begin flowing in the love of God toward others. The process of being healed emotionally is the process of dying to self so that Christ may live through us. The process of freeing the Lavatera tree is the same process used to free wounded, emotionally broken and bound people. Like the root bound tree some separation will be needed to allow the person to flourish.

But the separation is done gently, strategically and in love so that the person is helped not damaged.

"Blessed are the pure in heart; for they shall see God" (Matthew 5:8). Every transaction with God is a heart transaction. What has manifested in our lives is a result of the condition of our hearts. Our problem behaviors result from the problems in our hearts. The things that come out of the mouth come from the heart. The process of cleansing starts from the inside out. "For out of the heart come evil thoughts, murder, adultery, sexual immorality, false testimony and slander. These are what make a man unclean" (Matthew 15:18-20).

In Psalm 139:23-24 King David wrote: "Search me, O God, and know my heart, test me and know my anxious thoughts. See if there is any offensive way in me, and lead me in the way everlasting." Our similar prayer will invite the Holy Spirit to begin the restoration process. By allowing the Holy Spirit to reveal our heart and mind we can see if there is anything contrary to the truth of God in us. The Holy Spirit will expose beliefs that are contrary to the truth about God, about us, and about others. These false beliefs are ghosts and shadows that keep us from seeing who Jesus really is and from becoming who God created us to be. "As a man thinks in his heart, so is he" (Proverbs 23:7a).

If we believe lies about God then we are open to blaming Him for our distress. He is not an angry judge waiting for us to make a mistake so he can punish us. He is not a hard taskmaster demanding service. He is not a distant God too important and too busy to be concerned with the details of our lives. He is a good God who desires intimate relationship with us. He is a kind, loving, giving, and a personal God who very much wants to bless, protect, and comfort us. He wants us to come out of the shadows.

The Process

When we acknowledge our need for a Savior and accept the gift provided to us by the Heavenly Father in sending Jesus to be that Savior; the spirit of Jesus, which is the Holy Spirit, comes into our human spirits and we are born again. At that moment our spirits are perfect before God. We have been made the righteousness of God in Christ Jesus. However, our souls (mind, will, and emotions) and bodies did not change. If we were bald before we are still bald. If we were timid before that experience, we still feel timid. The process of sanctification is the application of the truth of God to our souls and that application changes us to line up with who God intended us to be.

Healing prayer and deliverance are tools the Holy Spirit uses to make salvation fully effective in all dimensions of our life and character. It is the application of the crucified and resurrected life of Jesus and the power of His blood applied to those parts of our soul that have not yet been sanctified. Inner healing and deliverance are a process, not a moment. They bring insight into why we do what we do or feel what we feel. It does not however, leave us at the threshold of understanding but takes us through the door of change.

Acknowledging that something is wrong happens when a person admits that their life is out of order, either in their emotional reactions, in their relationships, or in their choices. For example, anger as a reaction to a seemingly insignificant event, inability to stay in relationship with others, overeating, overworking, addictions, irrational fears, depression, and panic are all evidence that something is out of divine order. To recognize our plight is the first step to inner healing, freedom and spiritual growth.

The second level of awareness is realizing that someone or something is a substitute for God. Something else is giving us value or being used to fill us and give us a sense of worth. Jesus is the only real person with living water and the only source of life. When we attach the thirst that belongs to Him alone onto someone or something else, we eventually dry up because we are choosing to go to broken containers that can hold no water. Idolatry becomes painful when our attachment begins to produce death in us.

This brings us back to the issue of what is in our hearts. Emotions are a signpost indicating what is in our hearts. Positive feelings motivate us toward good, toward love and passion for God. Negative feelings motivate us toward evil; they cripple our will and move us away from God.

By understanding our feelings, we can connect with the root of what is in our hearts. Negative heart attitudes are what scripture calls strongholds. These strongholds keep us bound to negative emotions and negative behavior. The weapons that God had given us to pull down these strongholds are not of the flesh, but spiritual and mighty through God and will pull them down completely (2 Corinthians 10:5).

Some types of strongholds are:

- **Vows** - Decisions regarding specific aspect of relationships, usually involving the need to stay safe or be in control.
- **Perversions** – Abnormal desires that reflect a knitting together of experience, feeling and sexual energy other than how God ordained them to be.
- **Fortresses** – Ways of thinking and acting that form safe places to hide.

- **Faulty Beliefs** – Beliefs about the world that have been generalized from specific wounding events or dysfunctional family cultures.
- **Idolatrous Attachments** – Beliefs about the ability of the creation as the source of life, usually resulting in compulsive attachment to a person or an object.

Inner healing is the process of turning to the Lord and allowing Him to shine His light into the deepest parts of our souls to show us what is going on there. As we confess and repent at a heart level, barriers to the knowledge of God and relationship with God are removed. Restoration is not possible until we acknowledge the darkness and yield to the light (truth). To be free of the bondage it is imperative that we engage our will and turn to the Lord with our whole heart. Whenever a person turns to the Lord and asks for truth, the veil is taken away. "Now the Lord is a Spirit, and where the Spirit of the Lord is, there is freedom" (2 Corinthians 3:16-18). The Lord does not look at the things man looks at. Man looks at the outward appearance, but the Lord looks at the heart. The persons praying with you and for you are intended to facilitate the work of the Holy Spirit in shining His light of revelation into your soul. As the vows, strongholds, faulty beliefs, and bondages are exposed the person is aided in the forgiveness or repentance process. These transactions are between the person seeking restoration and the Lord. It is the Holy Spirit who brings the transformation and restoration. Those present are to be instruments in the hand of the Lord to love the person through the process to freedom and wholeness.

Hindrances to Healing

- Unwillingness to be open and honest before God
- Unwillingness to submit to the Word of God
- Unwillingness to repent and let go of sin
- Unforgiveness

Our part is to cooperate with the Holy Spirit as He leads us in the way that we should go and yield to His way of being and doing life.

CHAPTER 4

CROSSING THE THRESHOLD

(Irma's story)

One would think that a cold floor in a dark room would not be very comforting but for Irma it was a great refuge. Each night after everyone was asleep, she would tiptoe into the bathroom and lock the door. Sleeping on the floor mat covered with a bath towel was safer than the threat of her uncle coming to her bed in the wee hours of the morning.

He was a large man who wore heavy black army boots and reeked of cheap cologne. His large groping hands matched his large bulging eyes. He had served a few tours overseas and came to live in their home for a few months until he got settled as a civilian. On that terrible night Irma woke up to find his fat body on top of her small frame. She was frozen under his weight. She gasped for air as he groped at her with his hands and mouth.

She was drowning in the smell of alcohol unable to scream. He tried to rape her but was too drunk. Terror gripped her with a force stronger than his lust. He threatened to kill her if she uttered a word to anyone. The following day she was nauseated and in shock but devised a plan to keep him from her bed. That night after everyone was asleep, she slipped into the bathroom and locked the door. She could not remember how many nights she had slept on the bathroom floor, but remembered the day he moved out of her home. Irma stayed in bed that night and cried herself to sleep with tears of relief. She decided no one would ever hurt her like that again. She became somber, angry and hardened.

Locking herself in the bathroom was her way of coping as a very frightened eleven-year-old. Stress is a muscle spasm of the mind and Irma was severely stressed. She could not eat or sleep and her eyesight became seriously impaired. She walked around in a blur, was stressed to the point of exhaustion and confused about her parents. Why did they allow him to live in our home? Why did he pick her out of all her sisters? At night she had trouble sleeping or would sleepwalk. During the day she was constantly looking over her shoulder. She isolated herself and depression was her constant companion. Irma vacillated between being a victim and being a hunter. She either went into hiding or was on vigilant alert for danger. No peace, no rest, no sense of security. At age thirteen she joined a neighborhood gang in an effort to protect herself at school and on the street. She projected a tough exterior while internally she was terrified.

At age sixteen Irma was sick and while in a high fever broke the vow of silence about the attempted rape. Her mother was horrified but her concern was not for Irma but for her uncle.

She did not want her husband to know about the incident for fear that he would kill her brother. Irma was devastated by her mom's lack of compassion or comfort. The message Irma got by her mom's response was that her brother was more important than her daughter. So, the secret went on.

Irma's father was a hardworking man with many mouths to feed. He often worked two jobs and ruled his house with an iron fist. Irma knew that he loved her but she could never please him. She could never get it right, say it right or make it come out right. He was demanding, critical and exploded with anger at the least provocation. Perhaps her mother was right and she was protecting her father from his own rage but she got lost in all of it and never did connect with either of them. Irma decided that authority figures would never hear her or help her so she stopped asking. At age seventeen she survived another attempted rape. She was assaulted at a friend's home. This time she kicked and screamed. She was rescued when someone heard her fist pounding on the wall, came in and knocked her assailant out cold. Irma became defiant and lived in a constant ping pong game between fighting to survive and wanting to die.

Irma experienced real trauma, pain and loss but she made a bitterroot judgment against her parents and hated men. She lived as a victim because of her expectation that no one would ever put her first, love her, help her or protect her. Twenty-one years after that first trauma Irma had an encounter with God that changed everything. Bankrupt for comfort, peace and love she was suddenly faced with the truth of the gospel and realized that someone did love her. Loved her enough to die for her, to take her sorrows and her tears, her pain and weaknesses. Irma asked Jesus to help her and heal her. This time someone heard her, this time someone came to her rescue and helped her. Irma's healing process took time and many prayer and deliverances sessions but it started with that one decision.

In her first healing prayer session she closed my eyes and saw herself on the floor in that cold dark bathroom. Suddenly the door opened and a great light flooded the room. Jesus was standing on the other side of the threshold extending His hand to her. She took His hand and stepped across the threshold. As she stepped out, He said to her "If you ever find yourself in that dark room again it will be because you chose to go back to it. I want you to stay in the light with Me."

The dark room and cold floor represented Irma's desperate efforts of self-preservation. It took many more prayer session to process through all that had happened. She had altered her life in order to cope with the trauma of her childhood and that also needed to be made right. The Holy Spirit was patient and took her slowly and calmly through each event and each decision and their consequences until she was healed and free. The deep internalized emotional pain had manifested in infirmity and as her soul was healed her weak body was also healed and strengthened.

When we are in emotional pain it is that we have a need that has not been met. We have a right to expect our needs to be met by God. People will fail us because of their own wounding. But Jesus will always meet us with comfort and unconditional love. If you have been hiding in darkness, I invite you to take that crucial step and cross the threshold. Jesus will take your hand and walk you into His marvelous light.

"My soul has escaped as a bird from the trap of the hunter. The trap is broken and I have escaped. My help is in the Lord, who made heaven and earth" (Psalm 124:7-8).

CHAPTER 5

ORPHAN

(Tracy's Story)

The sobs are so deep that I am convulsing without making a sound. I started out hating them but somewhere along the way I misplaced my anger and turned it inward against myself. The taproot has to come out so that I can walk out of this dark corridor. Everything is twisted and my perception of right and wrong seem to bring me great pain. I am continually misunderstood and my words and intent are twisted. All I can do is turn to God and ask him to remove it or change it, whatever "it" is.

It was the right way, the wrong way and his way. If I objected to "his way" he got angry and turned me away. There was no dialogue because I had no right to object. Not his doing, not his fault, not guilty. My dad always justified himself to himself and then it became someone else's problem. He walked away drunk and untouchable. My mom was so out of touch with reality that dialogue was impossible. Her escape was a room to which there was no key.

My dad was an alcoholic and my mom suffered from mental illness. I convinced myself that I had to be perfect or I would turn out like one of them. I lived in a cycle of despair because I could never do it all perfectly. My dad escaped into alcohol and my mom into a demented world that did not exist. I could endure the loneliness more than the pain of seeing them destroy each other. I am not sure if I cried over their pain or over their sin. Most days I just wanted to unplug the cord and disconnect from their turmoil.

When I was eight the state unplugged the cord and I was sent to a foster home and then to another three years later. The second couple was very nice and I slowly started to feel safer. I especially got attached to the husband who was a kind man and seemed to want to hear what I had to say. Two years later they were killed in a boating accident and I was devastated and in anger shut my heart. I was bounced from home to home never making any lasting relationships. I went through the motions and was obedient on the outside but inside I was rebelling against every authority figure and especially against God. I managed to graduate from high school but what I had learned was that love never lasts and people always go away. I always had to take a number and wait in line with little hope that my number would even be called.

At age nineteen I was date raped and shut down for the next ten years. I struggled to hold on to my mental health and went from job to job living a solitary life just like I had as a child. I had to make hard choices alone and the grief never lifted. Somehow the isolation that had helped me survive as a child was not working for me. I was walking around like a dead person with no purpose and no connection to another human soul. I felt like I had always been an orphan.

Tracy heard the gospel and invited Jesus to come into her heart. It was not an easy decision, as her heart had no room for another abandonment. But by grace through faith her spirit was born again. She embraced the truth about Jesus being her savior but she had her doubts about this new life lasting. She especially had trouble connecting to the Heavenly Father. Life had told her she would never find lasting love because even her parents had abandoned her. She was an orphan, with no connection or revelation of love and affection. Rebellion had hooks in her soul and she had continued fighting with her dad long after he was gone. She now put his face on Father God and it kept her from trusting Him. Her years of pain and struggle had caused her to be independent and self-focused. Until her deep need for the Father's love was met, she would only experience a superficial relationship with Jesus. Only the love of the Father could displace the fear and only the truth of the Word of God could free her from the lies she had believed about herself.

When Tracy came in for inner healing and deliverance prayer, she was desperate but came with much hesitancy because she believed no one, including God, really wanted to help her or could meet her needs.

After sharing her history, she made one of the most important decisions of her life. Although the taste of dysfunction was still in her mouth she chose as an act of her will to forgive her birth parents and all the foster parents for what they had done to her and especially for what they had failed to do for her.

Suddenly she spit out the hollow empty sadness and she could breathe deeply and freely. It was the first step in her restoration process.

She spent the next year focused on the scriptures that addressed the truth of God's character and about his love for her as his daughter. In time she was able to forgive herself for blaming God for her hard life. She came to see that it was the sin nature of man that had caused her so much pain and not the Heavenly Father. The orphan who was afraid to love, trust and connect was slowly being healed and delivered. She came to understand that her parents could never give her what they themselves did not have and truly released them from their debt to her.

As Tracy yielded to being a daughter of the Heavenly Father joy sprung up in her soul. She had never experienced joy. She was a bit awkward in expressing it but soon adapted nicely. Intimacy with the Father birthed her true identity and allowed her to connect with others.

The orphan takes twelve steps down into the dark lonely tunnel and the way out is reversing those steps one at a time. The orphan sees the fault in the parents and gets hurt by them. They are affected by the pain and lose trust in parental authority. Fear sets in, especially the fear of receiving love and comfort. The hurt becomes solidified and the person believes they are a mistake. An independent spirit comes forth and they learn to conform outwardly and rebel inwardly. Performance becomes the rule, and superficial relationships form (meeting needs with no real connection). Lies form in their mind about themselves, God and others. The greatest lie is that there is no one who can meet their needs therefore they become self-focused and try to meet their own needs by looking for love in wrong places. Anywhere along this dark tunnel where God is allowed to intervene the person can get help. The love of God will displace the orphan spirit. As sonship is accepted the person can rest knowing that God the Father will help them, provide for them and never leave or forsake them. But it starts with a choice to accept the love of God and not put pain and suffering above God. He can re-parent the orphan if He is allowed to do so. Jesus walked on earth as a son before He became a savior and before He healed, preached or delivered anyone. Sons, not orphans, can experience intimate relationship, joy, peace and purpose. Creation is groaning and waiting for the sons of God to know their Father and embrace Him.

Tracy agreed to forgive, to take her eyes off her pain and her past and put them on Jesus. She agreed to allow the Heavenly Father to reveal himself to her and reparent her. She agreed to meditate on the scriptures focused on the love of God for her. She is no longer an orphan.

Forgiveness is a choice we make arising from our personal awareness that a blockage exists between us and God in the spiritual realm or between us and another person in the natural realm. Unforgiveness acts as a barrier to spiritual progress and will grossly inhibit our relationship with God and our fellow man.

Repentance starts the process, forgiveness completes the process and restoration is the result of the process. Unforgiveness has fruit. The fruit of this tree is worry, trouble, distress, suffering, unanswered prayer, sickness, holding a grudge, relational damage and the law of reversion. The law of reversion places us under the same issues of judgment, condemnation and un-forgiveness we choose to hold against another. It is like a boomerang and places us in spiritual prison. Chronic unforgiveness is related to a judgmental and jealous spirit within us. Unforgiveness is not the result of what another did or did not do or say, but the result of how we choose, consciously or unconsciously, to respond to another person's actions, words or inactions. In the process of forgiveness, we are letting go of judging others, condemning others and demanding retribution and therefore releasing ourselves from prison. Forgiveness is not a sign of weakness or an admission of wrongdoing. It is an act of obedience to God's directive.

If you have been living as an orphan, God is asking you to surrender to truth and to look at internal issues honestly yielding them to Him for healing instead of connecting with others who will agree with your victimization. You need healthy people who won't feed the self-pity and hold you accountable to the truth of the Word of God. The remedy is deep healing and restoration and it starts with humility by asking the Lord to heal you instead of being stubborn. Demonic rebellion feeds on real hurts and wrongs. It fixes its gaze on the problem so that the person will not pull back from how they were wronged and consequently stay in the wound. Pride covers the wound with activity and refuses to look in the mirror. Pride won't let you confront your own faults and dysfunction. Instead it continues to call right what God calls wrong. Even religious activity can be used to avoid truth and only truth will set you free and lead you to healing.

Jesus is a two-way door, a door into relationship with the Heavenly Father, which leads to peace, contentment, strength, health, and provision of every kind. Jesus is also a door out of guilt, shame, bitterness, insecurity and fear, sickness, weakness, poverty and lack. Jesus is a solid two-way door. Choose to enter into Jesus and leave the orphan behind.

"When my father and my mother forsake me then the Lord will take care of me" (Psalm 27:10).

"I will not leave you an orphan: I will come to you" (John 14:18).

CHAPTER 6

BOOT PRINT

(Norma's story)

My heart is pounding in my chest because of death's terrors. Fear has come upon me and I'm shaking at the core. One stronger than I forced his will upon me with absolutely no regard for me. I wish I had wings like a bird so that I could fly away and rest. I would run so far away; I would live in the desert. I would hurry to my hideout and escape this storm. If it had been an enemy that attacked me; then I could have understood it; if it had been one that hated me or magnified himself against me; then I would have hidden myself from him; but it was my mate, my close companion. We took sweet counsel together and walked into the house of God together. He put forth his hands against me although I was at peace with him, and he broke his covenant to protect me. The words of his mouth were smoother than butter, but war was in his heart. His words were softer than oil, yet they were drawn like a sword against me. But I have cast my burden upon the Lord and He has sustained me; He shall never allow me to be destroyed (Adapted from Psalm 55).

Some people walk with a limp or a cane as an obvious sign of their handicap. Others walk with a broken heart and a fractured soul. These are not visible to the eye but they are handicapped all the same. It is God's deepest desire to bring healing to one as much as to the other.

It had been six months since her company had relocated. Although the drive was longer the trees that line the longest stretch were worth seeing every morning. Norma thought she was settled into her new environment until one cold winter evening. Before leaving work, she went to the bathroom anticipating traffic on the way home. She had always felt uneasy in that bathroom but never could quite put her finger on why.

That night as she was washing her hands, she looked in the mirror and saw the pink and grey tile that lined the room. Suddenly she knew why she was so uneasy in that room. It was the same tile that had lined the shower rooms at the racquetball club. Seeing that tile triggered memories long ago buried and suddenly she had a meltdown. Although Norma had been divorced for many years she was still married to the pain of that relationship and there she sat on the floor with her head in her hands. She sobbed until there were no tears left to cry.

Two or three times a week they would use the racquetball club. They started out playing together but like everything else that did not last long. He played so hard and fast that she feared getting smacked by one of his zingers. He soon found a couple of men from work to play with and she would play alone. Late one evening she had just come out of the women's dressing room when he pulled her into the men's shower room. Before she knew what was happening, he had her shorts off and was forcing himself on her. There were a couple of men in the shower room but they ignored what was happening. They knew she was his wife so they must have figured things were okay. But he was raping her and no one protested, not even Norma. He was too strong, too violent and she was frozen in shock. It was not the sex he wanted. Somehow, she knew he was making some outrageous statement to himself or to the other two men about power, domination or his masculinity.

Norma never went back to the racquetball club. Perhaps that is what he really wanted. She didn't know and didn't care. She felt violated, betrayed and soiled. She was bleeding on the inside and nothing could explain or reason that away. It was the final straw in a long line of abusive behavior, days of being in dread and so many nights spent alone. That spirit of abuse and hatred of women that violated her in the racquetball club had left a large boot print on her soul. She shut down and went into a deep depression. Pain internalized, but she had to keep going. No time to process, heal or recover.

It was like a beautiful sea at first with the sunlight glistening on the surface of the water and reflections like diamonds in the fullness of the noonday sun. But suddenly the sun began to set and the shadows were cold. The winds blew and pierced her heart. Where did the sunlight go? Where did the comfort, warmth and beauty of the glistening water run? Who stole them from her? Norma tried to make her own fire, her own warmth, but her efforts were no match for the force of the cold winds and the wailing bitter darkness. The dark night of the soul was bitter and the dawn long in coming. Whatever fantasy she had about marriage had been utterly shattered.

Norma was devastated, humiliated and shamed. she hid herself by overworking and avoiding him. They never discussed the incident. No words could ever erase the negative imprint on her soul or explain his betrayal. With that boot print their marriage was crushed.

He thought she was his property and that he was entitled to sex however and whenever he wanted it regardless of how it damaged or traumatized her. She was sure his years of substance abuse had a part to play in his emotional insensitivity and egotism. The verbal degradation and devaluation were only trumped by his chronic brooding anger and mood swings. But there was no excuse for the psychological trauma that caused her to be frozen in fear and alone in the darkness of grief.

Better to have been alone than to be desperately isolated while in the company of another. She was lost in the dark. She dared not move for fear of falling off a cliff, or worse encountering him. The one that was the promised protector, provider and cherished companion had somehow turned out to be her bitter opponent lashing out at her in his pain. She waited for the dawn. She sat in silence, crying out in her heart for comfort and protection. The dawn never came so in the darkness she just slowly slipped away.

It had been a long time since that incident in the racquetball club and Norma was grateful that she no longer lived with that violent man, but she could still taste the grief. How could she feel really safe from the world around her and from the constant dread of sudden attack? Her body was the house she lived in and it had never been safe. The assaults always came either from him or from illness. In either case she had to fight to hold on to her house and recover her balance. She did not blame God for what happened to her. It was her choice to marry the man and his choice to violate her. His words and behavior were selfish, self-centered, controlling and abusive. He had harmed her mentally, emotionally, physically, spiritually and sexually.

God had sustained her. Now she asks Him to also restore her. Her prayer that night was that God would help her find the shadow of His wing that she might escape the emotional torment and be restored to soundness. She would understand what went wrong later, or perhaps never, but at that moment she just needed to feel safe and to know the reality of God's love and protection. The Bible says that the righteous run to the Lord, and are safe. Norma needed desperately to find that place in Him. So, she read and meditated on every scripture on the protection of the Lord. She clung to Jesus; her only true protector and her only hope. He never tried to control her or trick her. He never abused her or betrayed her. He never lied to her or threatened her. His love for her had never changed. Norma had forgiven therefore she had peace, now she looks to Him to bring her the joy that was long ago stolen.

Norma lived the truth of the words of the psalmist who wrote that it is better to be alone on the corner of a rooftop then in a large house with a violent man. By God's grace she honestly forgave her broken and tormented husband and released him to the Lord. Day by day, as she read the scriptures and worshiped God, the Lord's love and kindness healed her shattered heart.

But he was not the only one she had to forgive. Norma had a bitter hatred against herself for having chosen to marry the man and it resulted in her not being able to trust herself to make good choices. It took years, but by God's mercy she came to forgive herself. The twisted thinking was corrected by the power of the truth. Chief among the twisted thinking was that it was her fault, that sex at any cost was her marital obligation and that the problem was her inability to deal with his abuse. She forgave herself and then she broke the ungodly soul tie between them, and the cords of death that bound her to him. Such is the power of the Spirit of God to heal the layers of the soul.

Norma now lives in the reality of Psalm 91; Jesus is the shadow of the Almighty, the secret place that she runs to. He has dried her tears, and she can look with anticipation to another day trusting in His protection and anticipating joy because He is her hope and His mercies are new every morning. "Those that sow in tears shall reap in joy" (Psalm 126:5).

"Who have I in heaven but You? And there is none upon earth that I desire besides You. My flesh and my heart fail: But God is the strength of my heart and my portion forever" (Psalm 73:25-26).

CHAPTER 7

UNCLEAN

(Eva's story)

He yelled and called me a rotten kid, but when mom was gone, he didn't act like I was rotten. He told me I was soft and sweet. The verbal abuse was to keep me scared and quiet. The double talk was to keep me confused and intimidated.

The first time was the worst. The room was open and full of light when he entered. Suddenly the door was locked and the lights went out. The world was locked out. Everything I had ever known to be beautiful and peaceful was shut out and I became locked in an internal emotional darkroom. I went dead inside. I was ruined.

What my dad wanted was a toy, a centerfold. I became nothing but a doll, a piece of meat for his pleasure. His threats were real. He made sure I knew they were real. I slept a lot. That's how I escaped when I could not bear the numbing pain and anger. While other teenagers were reading Bodice Rippers and fantasizing in their minds, I was living it out and hating every moment, every touch, every smell.

When I was fourteen, I had the body of a seventeen-year-old and could not escape the fact that boys and men alike undressed me in their minds. I could think of nothing but my body. I felt no shame at knowing how to make a guy go wild with lust. I was actually proud that I was soiled. Is that a kick? I was full of slime and thought it was beautiful.

The older I got the more jealous my dad became. He wanted to control every minute of my life. At sixteen I got fed up with him and ran away from home. I had no trouble finding guys to take me in. The best part was that now I could stay buzzed all the time. All they wanted in exchange was sex. There are lots of days I can't remember between the ages of sixteen and nineteen as one-night stands and six-month lovers all blurred together. I ended up in the hospital a few times unable to say what had happened to me because I was stoned.

At age twenty I met a man who was older and seemed to like me. He was cute and it was obvious he had money but somehow, he wouldn't come on to me. I couldn't figure him out. What did he want if he did not want my body?

He invited me to have dinner with him and took me to a really nice hotel. I figured we'd have dinner and then I would be the dessert. When we got inside, he took me to a banquet room and we sat with some people he obviously knew. We had dinner and then a man got up and spoke. He told how he had been the CEO of a big company and lost everything including his family because of alcohol. He ended up broke, alone and suicidal. Then he met a man in a park who told him that God loved him even though he knew every disgusting thing he had ever done. By that time, I was crying and my head was fuzzy because I hadn't had a drink or a hit for a few hours. I wanted to run out of there but I felt like someone had glued me to the chair. I noticed that the guy who had brought me had a big smile on his face. He seemed to be "flying" but he hadn't used anything.

When the speaker got finished telling how Jesus had taken him out of the gutter and gotten him back on his feet he asked if anyone wanted Jesus to do the same for them. To my amazement I walked up to where he was crying and shaking like a leaf. I know there were other people around me but I could not really see well because I was crying so hard. Suddenly I was disgusted with myself and wanted to die. I felt like everyone in that room knew every dirty thing I had ever done. I remember thinking "I am a filthy wreck and I want to die." Then I heard the man say. "Ask Jesus to wash you clean and make you whole again." I wanted that, I needed that. I felt like everything had been my fault and I needed to be punished. Then I heard him say, "Jesus has paid the price your sins deserve. Your fine has been paid in full." I gave my dirty, trashy life to Jesus and at that moment I felt a warm peace come into my heart.

Like a dress fallen off the hanger I was crumpled and down-trodden on the ground. I could not pick myself up and put myself back on the hanger. I needed a man humble enough to pick me up and strong enough to hang me back up on the rack of life. A man who could clean me up and take me to a higher place and restore my dignity. The only man who could go that low and reach that high is Jesus. He allowed himself to go to hell where

I belonged so that He could raise me up to sit with Him at the right hand of the Father and live with Him forever. For the very first time in my life I felt clean and suddenly everything around me looked crystal clear.

Since that night I have had a lot of changes. I moved into a women's home, finished high school and learned what the Bible says about love, real love and forgiveness. I have gone through inner healing and deliverance. At first it was really hard. I didn't think I belonged there. I didn't know how to live without a man or how to ask for what I needed without expecting to pay with sex. It was hard to accept kindness from people. I thought they would change if they knew about my past. They didn't ask, I guess they already knew. It took months before I could open up.

These people actually wanted to know how I felt and what I needed. My dad told me I had no right to speak. Suddenly I had a voice but I was not sure what people would do if they heard what I had to say. The more I read the Bible the worse I felt. Shame covered my face because I had done all those wicked ugly things called "sin". When I would get that way, I wanted to sleep a lot, just like when I was a kid. Thankfully the counselors talked with me and prayed with me. Slowly all the trash of my childhood got sorted out. I learned I had an ungodly soul tie with my dad and with every other man I had slept with and that there were cords of death that came with each of them. The only way to freedom was to ask God to forgive me, to forgive them and to cut those soul ties and the cords of death.

I learned that a soul tie is a knitting together of two souls and that those ties work for good or for evil. The strongest soul ties are with sexual partners and especially the first sexual partner. In my case that was my dad, and incest formed an ungodly soul tie between us. Once it was pointed out to me, I could see soul ties in the stories of the Bible. Like David and Jonathan, Ruth and Naomi, Abraham and Sarah. They had godly soul ties and were knit together in a good way. They drew strength and encouragement from each other like the new Christians in Acts 4 that were of one heart and one soul. But Herodias and Herod, Jezebel and Ahab, Samson and Delilah were all knit to each other in ungodly soul ties. Saul was tied to David through hatred and jealousy, Tamar and her brother were knit together in an ungodly way through his lust for her and the rape. He told her he loved her but his love hurt her and shamed her. She came away damaged and rejected. Just like my dad had done to me.

My dad and I already had a soul tie as father and daughter but his abuse, control and intimidation were selfish and his love toxic. It was poison to my soul. The incest bound us and the secrecy compounded the perversion. His soul was knit to mine through lust for power, control and sex, as were those of every other man I had ever been with. Each man I had sex with took a fragment of my soul until I was splintered. The ungodly cord that connected my soul to my dad was the strongest and it had me bound to men and sex in demonic cords of fear, anger, intimidation, abuse, sexual perversion, death, and hatred of men. Instead of being knit together in pure love we were knit together in sexual perversion. I was caught up internally with him. As much as I hated what he had done to me I could not stop focusing on it. It consumed my thoughts and I drank and used drugs to escape the crazy thinking. I thank God that we can cut ungodly soul ties and recover the fragments of our souls. Jesus, who is my Good Shepherd, has restored my soul.

If you have had an ungodly soul tie, not just a sexual one but any knitting of your soul to another person in an ungodly way you can be free. Psalm 7:2 describes the soul as being torn by a lion tearing it in pieces. That was my soul. Nothing tears the soul like perverted sex.

Thank God for providing a way for the restoration of our souls through the Blood of Jesus. Begin the healing by admitting that an ungodly soul tie exists. Forgive the person for what they have done and ask forgiveness for your part and your reaction to what was done to you. Then ask the Lord to cut that unholy soul tie and send back to the person, through the Blood of Jesus, what belongs to them (their anger, lust, jealousy, blame, control, etc.) and take back to yourself, cleansed through the Blood of Jesus, what belongs to you (dignity, purity, peace and joy etc.). Finally ask the Lord to release His holy fire to break any cords of death between you (death to your relationships, marriage, emotions, mental and physical health etc.). Cut the cords that bind you to depression, betrayal, mental illness, oppression, and suicide.

The destroyer brings terror. He gains access to a life because of a lack of godly protection. Once victimized a shield of self-protection keeps emotions hidden, locked up in a room of internal bondage. The Holy Spirit has the key to each room but our part is to allow Him to use it and to yield to the healing process. That process always includes forgiveness which leads us out of the house of bondage. If we are obedient to forgive God's mercy will always triumph over judgment. He will deal with perpetrators; our part is to turn them over to Him.

Jesus came to set captives free, to heal broken hearts and to cleanse lepers. He has done it all for me and I will forever be grateful to Him. The Bible says that the soul is purified by obedience to the truth. The truth is we do not have to stay in bondage. Jesus came to set us free (1 Peter 1:22).

Jesus said He is the way the truth and the life. Faith in Jesus Christ brings us into covenant relationship with the Heavenly Father and out of the bondage to sin. It gives us courage to come out of fear and rejection and into acceptance. I acknowledged Jesus as my Savior and Lord and stepped out of hatred and shame into forgiveness and cleansing. I invite you to step into Jesus who loves you and wants to cleanse you and restore to you all that has been stolen from you.

CHAPTER 8

FEAR FACTOR

(Sarah's story)

Awake or asleep Sarah could never rest. Fear and anxiety ruled her life. Everything was a cause for worry. What had brought her to this pitiful condition?

She was a sick and frail child and as a teen men and women alike had intimidated, oppressed and abused her. She was afraid of everything and everyone. At age 19 she married a man who was in the medical community thinking that he would be her protector, only to find that he was selfish and indifferent. Instead of protecting her, he tried to dominate her. The battle for control was unending and his drinking only pushed her farther and farther into fear and isolation.

Two years after their divorce she came to know and accept the Lord Jesus Christ and one of the first issues he addressed in her life was fear. The first scripture she memorized was Isaiah 41:10 that reads: "Fear not for I am with you; look not anxiously about you for I am your God. I will help you; I will strengthen you and I will lift you up with My righteous right hand."

She loved the comfort of the scriptures and was faithful to read them daily and attend church each week. Slowly she began to feel safer and her guard began to drop. But the intent of her lifelong menaces of fear was to keep her bound to what her experiences said she was, a victim. The enemy of her soul did not want Sarah to be at peace. He had a stronghold in her life and wanted to keep it. So, he set an assignment against her right in the place she felt the safest.

A man in the church she was attending started to stalk her. Everywhere she turned he was there. If she moved during the service soon, she would see him nearby. If she moved to the choir loft, he would soon follow. She decided to serve in the children's ministry for a few months in an effort to avoid him and in hopes that his attention would be turned elsewhere. Late one night she looked out her living room window and saw him parked outside her home. Fear kicked into high gear and she panicked. Instead of picking up the phone to call for help she started barricading the doors and nailing the windows shut. When she finally picked up the phone and called for help, he was gone. The next day she reported the incident to her pastor and to the police. Their investigation revealed that he had done the same thing to three other women. He never hurt them; he just frightened them. He was suspended from the church and sent to psychiatric therapy.

Over the next six months the Lord worked with Sarah to disarm those triggers and heal the memories of her life that had predisposed and trained her to react to every situation with apprehension. He truly was helping her, strengthening her and upholding her. As she continued in her battle against fear the Lord proved to her over and over again that the scenarios of her childhood could be disarmed as he took her from one situation to another delivering her and proving that he was faithful to protect her and provide help for her in times of trouble.

After six months Sarah ran into the man who had stalked her in the parking lot of a supermarket and to her surprise she was not triggered. She looked him straight in the eye and asked him why he had stalked her. His sheepish reply was that he was only trying to scare her. She told him he had succeeded but that she wanted to understand what twisted pleasure he got out of it. He reported that his former wife had tried to stab him in his sleep and he somehow enjoyed making women as frightened as he had been when he awoke to find a knife at his throat. He admitted he had been wrong and asked for forgiveness. Sarah forgave him and they parted ways.

The following year Sarah was diagnosed with rheumatoid arthritis. The doctor recommended she move to a dry climate, as there was no hope for remission or a cure. Visions of total disability loomed over her day and night. The physical pain and the anxiety were equally excruciating. One afternoon while sitting in her car she was overwhelmed with pain and she cried out to God for help. In that moment something like a bolt of electricity went through her from the top of her head to the tips of her toes. All the pain was gone and never returned. That was more than thirty years ago. The Lord took Sarah from one fear-inducing situation to another breaking down the walls of self-protection she had built around herself and proving she could trust Him to help her.

With each victory her faith in the Lord and her courage to stand against fear grew stronger. It is the Lord who gives us the power to confront and overcome our fears. One of those trials was when she was laid off her job. This time she did not panic and kept remembering God's faithfulness to her and his promise to be with her and help her. Within three weeks she was offered a better paying position, closer to home and with a nice group of people.

Fear and faith are alike in that they both have an expectation of something that has not yet happened, one for good, and the other for evil. The plumb line of Sarah's life was changing from fear to faith. She chose to focus her thinking on the truth that God is good and loves her. Fear does not come from him any more than sickness or sin comes from him. Fear is torment but Jesus told us not to be afraid because He has overcome fear.

"The Lord has not given us a spirit of fear but of power and love and a sound mind" (2 Tim 1:7). This statement in scripture clearly teaches us that fear is a demonic spirit and comes from Satan. When Adam and Eve sinned one of the first things that manifested in their lives was fear. Fear comes in through sin (ours, others or that of our ancestors) but Jesus came to deliver us from fear. "God is love and perfect love casts out fear. All who are led by the spirit of God are the children of God. For you have not received the spirit of bondage to fear but you have received the spirit of adoption whereby you call Abba, Father" (Romans 8:14-16).

God says to us "trust me" and a demon says "but what if...?" Listening to the demon we will eventually speak out "I am afraid I will lose my job, my child will get hurt, I'll get sick, my marriage will fail" etc. By speaking out you have used the power of your words to invite a spirit of fear to come in. Once in he will invite other spirits to join and strengthen him. The spirit of fear is a strongman (commander). Spirits attached to fear are torment, heaviness, depression, nightmares, heart attack, terror, phobias, etc. Fear is the gate-opener. Once open other spirits come in to bring oppression and cause torment. The ultimate goal of demons is to bring a person to insanity, suicide or early death. Because of fear of the future people are enticed into divination (fortune telling, tarot cards, astrology). Trauma causes people to escape in order not to remember and relive the trauma. Alcohol, drugs, overwork are all ways in which a person will try to escape both the trauma and the fear that came with it.

The way we deal with any demonic spirit is twofold, first by a truth encounter and a secondly by a power encounter. The truth encounter starts with being honest about our condition and then yielding to the truth of what God has said about it. There is no fear in love but perfect love casts out fear because fear has torment. He that fears is not made perfect in love (1 John 4:18). Repenting of fear (changing our mind, turning around and going the other way) is what will allow the process of change. The power encounter starts with forgiveness toward others and our own selves. Without forgiveness we cannot move forward. Once forgiveness has honestly been extended, we can bind the lie and loose the truth (Matthew 18:18). By immobilizing fear and releasing courage we are exercising authority. Calling on the name of Jesus, applying the power of His blood and establishing our faith in the finished work of the cross are the weapons of our warfare. We cast out the spirit of fear in the name of Jesus and forbid it to return.

Once free we must then resist fear each time it makes an effort to re-enter by using the word of God against it. We do this by opening our mouths and acknowledge that Jesus is our protector, provider, healer, etc. Jesus will become to us what we acknowledge Him to be. Fear of making a mistake will paralyze and cause anguish of soul. It will keep you stressed and uptight. If you get a bad medical report it will give you something specific to focus your prayer on. Acknowledge Jesus to be your healer, bind infirmity and refuse to accept whatever was diagnosed. Acknowledge Jesus as the strength of your life. Ask the Heavenly Father to release warring angels to do battle against the sickness and against the fear.

Pray this prayer as you forge your way through the battle against fear:

"I thank you Heavenly Father that I am your child and that you love me. In the name of Jesus, I declare that it is against my will to be afraid. I choose to reject the bondage and torment of fear. I choose to receive your love, power and a sound mind. According to Your word deliver me from all my fears that I may be made perfect in Your love. I ask You to disarm every trigger that brings fear and heal me of all intimidation. It is against my will to be sick and it is against my will to agree with death in any form. I choose life. Amen."

CHAPTER 9

CORE ISSUE

Following my conversion, I went through many months of inner healing and deliverance understanding that they were two sides of the freedom coin. Within a few years very concrete progress had been made. However, I still struggled in some areas and was frustrated.

One Saturday morning I asked the Lord to show me the core issue in my life. I stayed in bed and prayed for nearly an hour. Suddenly I saw in the spirit a banner across the room with the words "NO VALUE" written on it. The Lord was graciously answering my prayer. As I continued to pray in the Spirit, I came to understand that because of childhood trauma and having been mistreated and betrayed as a young adult I had come to believe the lie that I had no value.

The assaults of life had caused me to see myself as inferior and to believe that everyone else and their needs were more important than mine. But he began to show me that by the work of the cross and the power of the Holy Spirit I had the hope of being emotionally healed and having my mind renewed to the truth. The power to overcome is in the kingdom of God and the kingdom of God is within me because the Spirit of Jesus is in my heart. Your kingdom come; your will be done on earth as it is in heaven starts with me. The place the two kingdoms meet is found in intimacy with God. Being alone, vulnerable, and completely transparent before Him is where the transformation is found.

I sat straight up in bed and proceeded to come out of agreement with the lie that I had no value. I knew Jesus valued me enough to die for me. I asked the Lord to heal me and to renew my mind to the truth about my value. I wanted to see myself the way He saw me and to have divine order in my thinking.

The Apostle Paul wrote that we are chastened and yet not killed, sorrowful, yet always rejoicing, poor yet making many rich, having nothing, yet possessing all things. We are hard pressed on every side, yet not crushed, perplexed but not in despair, persecuted but not forsaken, struck down, but not destroyed. Always carrying about in our bodies the dying of the Lord Jesus that the life of Jesus may be manifest in our mortal bodies (2 Corinthians 4:10).

"Therefore, we do not lose hope and we do not lose heart. Even though our outward man is perishing, yet the inward man is being renewed day by day. For our light affliction, which is but for a moment is working for us a far more exceeding and eternal weight of glory, while we do not look at the things that are seen, but at the things that are not seen" (2 Corinthians 4:5-18). We are cast down but not destroyed.

Jesus said: "These things I have spoken to you, that in Me you may have peace. In the world you will have tribulation; but be of good cheer, I have overcome the world" (John 16:33). The trials will come, the test will come but he said not to be afraid of them because He has overcome them and we can overcome them because we are in Him and He is in us.

What that banner told me was that the core lie in my life was that I had no value. But the Holy Spirit has revealed to me the truth of who I am. I am of such great value that Jesus gave up everything so that I could be restored to the heart of the Father. I have value as His beloved child. I have favor with Him and He has made every provision for me. Since that day I take every situation that prompts a negative emotion or reaction in me and put it through the grid of truth. I ask myself: "How does this tell me that I have no value?" Then I deal with the lie by applying the truth to the situation.

Adversity will form us, not break us, if we trust in God's love for us. I asked Him to show me my value and who I am and what I could do and what I could be. He answered me with Romans 8:29, "For whom He foreknew, He also predestined to be conformed to the image of His Son, that He might be the firstborn among many brethren." He showed me that my destiny is to be conformed to the image of Jesus and that I am accepted and can have direct access to all He is. I am secure because I am no longer condemned and nothing and no one can separate me from His love for me. He chose me and I am preserved in Christ Jesus (Jude 1:1). No adversity has ever been able or will ever be able to destroy who I am in Christ Jesus.

When going through a test or trial, this five-step process will help you get the breakthrough:

First: Examine your heart because out of the heart come the issues of life.

According to Judges 2:22 the purpose of storms and trials is to test our hearts and teach us to do war. So, our part is to keep the weeds, rocks and foxes out of our hearts. They are unforgiveness, bitterness, offenses, grudges, jealousy and anger. The children of Israel cried out to the Lord and He always provided deliverance for them. Moses, Joshua, Gideon, Deborah, Joseph and David were all deliverers and types of the coming Messiah. Jesus is our deliverer. The Lord will use people and situation to search our hearts. His heart is always toward those who offer themselves willingly. In Judges 5 it says that when the people willingly offered themselves the Lord delivered them. When they finally yielded to the Lord, they had forty years of rest. All their enemies perished and all who loved the Lord were as the sun when it goes forth in his might.

Second: Do not be afraid. Be strong and of good courage.

"Though I walk through the valley of the shadow of death, I will fear no evil; for you Lord are with me. Your rod and your staff, they comfort me" (Psalms 23:4). His Word is the rod and the Holy Spirit is our comforter. Stay in the Word and call on the Holy Spirit. We are admonished 365 times in the Bible to not be afraid. He knew we would have to be reminded every day not to yield to fear.

Third: Be patient.

"Let patience have its perfect work, that you may be whole and entire lacking nothing" (James 1:4).

Joseph had a prophetic dream at the age of seventeen but he did not become Prime Minister until he was thirty. David was anointed to be king at the age of seventeen but was not crowned king until he was thirty. Each man had to wait thirteen years for the promise to be fulfilled. Abraham was promised a son would be born to him through Sarah. He had to wait twenty-five years for that promise to be fulfilled. None of them quit. Paul did not quit despite many hardships. Peter did not quit. He denied he even knew Jesus but later repented to God and was restored. Judas did quit. He tried to undo his betrayal of Jesus by repenting to the religious leaders and then he hung himself. If you miss it, admit it, run to Jesus, repent, receive his forgiveness and move on.

Fourth: Pray over and speak to your soul

Speak to your soul as David did when he said "Bless the Lord oh my soul and forget none of his benefit" (Psalm 103:1).

Ask the Lord to cleanse all the layers of your soul and to then fill each layer with His life, light, joy and peace. Talk to your soul and say "Mind, line up with the Word of God. Will, I command you to yielded to the Heavenly Father just as Jesus did, emotions stabilize." Remember that He who is creator of heaven and earth loves you.

At the start of every day decree and declare that it is against your will to be afraid. "The Lord is my light and my salvation; whom shall I fear? The Lord is the strength of my life of whom shall I be afraid? When I sit in darkness the Lord will be a light to me" (Micah 7:8).

"When I pass through the waters the Lord will be with me, and the rivers will not drown me. When I walk through the fire,

I will not be burned, and the flame will not scorch me. The Lord is my Savior" (Isaiah 43:2-3).

Fifth: Do not give up or let go.

Once I was doing yard work and used a chain saw to cut the branch of a lemon tree. The blade hit a knot in the branch and suddenly kicked the saw back. For a moment I lost my grip and the saw nicked my forearm. The material used to sew up the wound was not disposable. I was to go back in a few days to have the stitches removed. I waited over a week and consequently was left with a scar. My spiritual lesson from that situation was to hold on tightly to Jesus and pay attention to what I am doing so I will not experience backlash.

It is not the responsibility of the sheep to clean himself. He presents himself to the shepherd for inspection and the shepherd cleans him. Jesus is our Good Sheppard. We can't heal, restore or set ourselves free. He does it. Spiritual experience is not the goal. The goal is to become like Jesus. The healing comes from heaven. We are to engage heaven by presenting ourselves to Jesus who is our healer. If you do miss it and get hit run to Jesus immediately and allow Holy Spirit to take out the arrows, pins or daggers right away. Do not try to tough it out. Humble yourself to admit you made a mistake and get help.

Say continually: *"It is against my will to give up, quit or cave in. I choose to receive all the grace and mercy the Lord Jesus has provided for me. I will not lose heart. He never gives up on me and I will never give up either. I yield to the anointing of victory in Christ Jesus."*

CHAPTER 10

PRECIOUS JEWEL

(Elena's story)

While still in her mother's womb Elena was given a heart-shaped box that contained a perfectly shaped jewel. Her box looked like that of every other child but the color of the gem inside was uniquely hers. In all of creation there was not another jewel the shape or color of her jewel because it contained the core of what the Creator intended her to be. The evil one saw her gift and set a plan in motion to destroy it.

She was four months old when an infection attacked her body. To make matters worse, she was mistakenly given formula full strength and it damaged her digestive tract. Unable to retain any nourishment she was soon at the verge of starvation. Within days Elena was too weak to cry and lay listless in her mother's arms. In desperation her parents took her to an herbalist as they cried out to God for help. In His great mercy her life was spared as she slowly recovered on rice milk and chicken broth but she was left a frail and sickly child. The first black stones of weakness and infirmity had been placed in her heart-shaped box.

By the time Elena was six she had heard her parents argue so much that she lived in constant dread of the next explosion. The day came when her dad left home slamming the door as he stormed out of the house vowing never to return. She hid under the ironing board as tears streamed down her face convinced that she would never see him again. A few days later he returned, but abandonment and grief had already made their way into her heart. Too young to understand or fight the strategy, the enemy orchestrated events year by year that inserted black stones into her heart. First, they were sent to cover but ultimately with the intent of crushing her precious life.

Four years later her brother died in a car accident and she was nauseated with shock at the loss. She was swimming in confusion and the pain was intolerable. Elena ultimately decided that it was not safe to get close to anyone. She became somber, angry and distant. Her parents were broken with grief. Her dad started drinking and her mom escaped into prescription drugs. They had little energy to deal with her introversion and depression. Unable to concentrate her grades suffered. She hated her life and herself. Fear, anger and grief were now heavy boulders in her ten-year-old heart.

A few years later her family moved. A teacher at her new school saw beyond Elena's somber exterior and spoke kindly to her. She spent hours helping her and slowly her grades improved. She got involved in volleyball and helped design the school yearbook. With the help of this God sent angel Elena managed to graduate from high school.

Determined to be independent she got a part-time job and escaped into community college life. She was enjoying her freedom until an afterschool party turned into a nightmare. She was dancing up a storm when a guy she had never met pulled her into a bedroom and tried to rape her. Elena kicked and screamed with all her might. She was not going to take this without a fight. Someone finally heard her screams over the blaring music and knocked the assailant out cold. All the old emotions and fears got stirred up. She didn't want to deal with the memories so she started drinking to dull the emotional pain. Life became a string of hangovers and failed classes. The stones of offense no longer fit in her heart-shaped box. She now carried a backpack on her shoulder.

When Elena was twenty-years-old, she met a man who was in the Marines. His uniform convinced her that he would defend and protect her. He did not deceive her she deceived herself. She married someone she did not really know because she longed to escape her family life. Now she convinced herself that children would fill the emptiness that gnawed at her. It did not take long before the same arguing she hated to hear as a child was going on in her own marriage. To her surprise her husband had some wounds of his own and they hurled stones at each other day and night. Making more money, buying a bigger house and expensive vacations did not change a thing. After ten years of fighting they divorced. Elena had turned the backpack in for a heavy trunk filled with resentment and bitterness.

Dragging the weight of that trunk around drained her of hope. She had a recurring dream of a small lizard trapped in a dark room gasping for air. The lizard ran from one end of the room to another but there were no windows and no door. It became exhausted and would fall on the floor unable to breath. Alcohol and prescription drugs no longer satisfied her need to escape the nagging thought that her life was ruined. One night she took an overdose and would have slept her way into eternal hell had a neighbor not found her. It was on the bedroom floor in the dullness of her depression that she told Elena of someone who could help her out of the dark room with no door. Day by day she listened and prayed with her. Elena poured out her grief, confusion and anger. Her neighbor would patiently listen and then gently insert the truth of the love of God into her parched soul. Elena came to realize that God had not killed her brother and God had not caused her parents to fight or allowed her to be assaulted. She finally asked God to forgive her for blaming Him for everything and for wanting to die. She asked Jesus to pull her out of the dark room and take her back to her core.

Since that prayer Elena has been coming to Jesus day after day and He has been removing one stone of offense at a time. They do it together. She releases the stone through forgiveness and He removes it and heals the wound that was inflicted. She does not pretend that harm was never done; but instead chooses to release the person from the debt they owe her. She turns the issue of recompense and vengeance over to the Lord to deal with. By refusing to hold on to the stone that was hurled at her or to throw it back at the one who injured her she releases herself from the pain and torment. Only in acknowledging that God has forgiven her can Elena receive the grace to forgive others as well as herself. It has been through the power of forgiveness that Elena found the door to freedom. The Holy Spirit said to her "Jesus came in mercy and He is truth. We must clean each wound. Truth is the scalpel by which the poison and debris can be released and extracted. Mercy is the oil that soothes and comforts the wound so it can heal. Mercy and truth administered together will bring a full recovery."

There are still stones to be removed but over time enough restoration has been done to uncover the original jewel that makes Elena uniquely the person God created her to be. Because Jesus bore her scars on the cross of Calvary, He understands the pain and sorrow they brought her and how marred and distorted her self-image became as a result. Each day He allows her to see another facet of who He really is and who she is because He lives in her and belongs to Him. Just as the tree is in the seed the power is in the core. Elena has chosen to allow her seed to grow by watering it daily with the Word of God.

The book of Romans tells us that our destiny is to be conformed to the image of Christ. We all have the same destiny. However, we each have a different purpose. Restoration is the process that allows us to reach both our destiny and our purpose. Close your eyes and look into your heart. Can you see your gemstone or are there black stones covering it? Are you carrying a backpack or trunk full of scars and pain? If you have never brought those stones to Jesus you can do it now. Ask Him to take your heart and heal the wounds and fill it with his love. Jesus will pour His oil of healing over your wounds until your heart is whole and filled with His peace. He will lead you day by day until you come to see yourself the way He sees you...with favorable eyes, eyes of love and compassion...a beautiful jewel in his crown.

"You shall be a crown of glory in the hand of the Lord, and a royal diadem in the hand of your God" (Isaiah 62:3).

Prayer of Forgiveness:

"Heavenly Father, creator of heaven and earth, I come to You in the name of Jesus. As an act of my will and in obedience to Your word, I choose to forgive everyone who has sinned against me. I ask that You forgive me for all I have done against others, against myself and against You. I ask You to forgive me, and all my ancestors for any involvement in witchcraft, the occult and sexual sin. I forgive and bless those who have cursed me or abused me. I release them to You. I forgive those who have judged me and ask You to break their words and their judgments off of my life. I forgive myself for all I have done and all that I have failed to do. Please forgive me if I have blamed You for what others have done to me. Thank You for sending Jesus so that He could make a way for me to be healed and restored. I thank You for Your love, grace, and great mercy toward me. Help me to become like Jesus and show me exactly what my unique purpose is. Amen."

PART B

ALLEGORY OF
THE MOUSE

CHAPTER 11

THE PIT

"What's the point? No one can hear you and no one cares. No one will miss you." This was the taunt of the spider and the worm; constant, haunting and cruel. The little white mouse had fallen into a pit and these two were his constant companions. They could not hurt him physically but their words were like arrows to his soul. "Stupid, clumsy, weakling." It went on and on.

No point trying to remember how I got here. What difference will it make? I am in this pit of depression and going back serves no purpose. Understanding how I got here will not get me out and I refuse to waste any energy taking vengeance on my tormentors.

It is dark and cold in this dingy hole. I have no food or water and I am confused. Perhaps I hit my head when I fell in here. I can't feel any pain because I am frozen with fear. I know I must do something, but what? If I wait, nothing will change. Waiting only prolongs the hard choice and compounds the problem. The only way out is up.

The blanket of self-pity felt comforting at first but now it wants to smother me. I must throw it off or I will be extinguished. Mustering all my physical forces, I run in circles, trying desperately to reach the top of the pit, only to fall exhausted to the bottom, demoralized and in despair. Over and over again I try, only to be met with failure. Logic has failed me, and I can't see any other way out. Each effort is met with stronger opposition and ugly taunts from my two companions. I keep gasping for air trying to wake myself from this nightmare. The robber of my soul has me pinned to the floor and creatures of the night are trying to suck the life out of me. They have heavy hands and harsh tongues. They yell out, "There is no hope, you can't get out. Just die. It is the only way to end the cycle."

I object to the verbal abuse and explain my dilemma, but my words evaporate. I am crying out for help but who can hear such a small voice. The cycle always ends in defeat. Performance leads to exhaustion and then to depression. What's the point? I am helpless to rescue myself. The only hope I have is in my power to choose. I must cry out to One greater than myself if I am to be rescued. "Please deliver me, O Lord. Hurry up and help me. Let them be ashamed and confounded who seek after my soul to destroy it; let them be driven backward and put to shame that wish me evil" (Psalm 40:13-14).

Still the taunting continues. I object strongly to the spider and the worm. I refuse to yield to their invitation of death. I choose life! I also choose to forgive them and to look away from the flash cards of my past failures. I will rest now and I will wait. Not for death, but for an answer from the only one who can hear the cry of my heart. Perhaps my Creator will have mercy on me and help me. I commit myself into His hands and wait. If I die, I will return to Him. If I live, He will have rescued me.

No longer in a bed of languishing, the little white mouse sleeps peacefully for the first time since having fallen into the pit. A ray of sunlight awakens him and as he looks up, he sees a vine has grown over the ledge of the pit. Hope leaps within him as he contemplates the upward cycle once again. He quietly considers the situation. Will the vine be strong enough to bear my weight? Can I get high enough to reach it? If I do, will I have the strength to grasp it? No matter the answer he determines that he asked for help and was sent a vine. He has nothing to lose by trying to reach it.

Resolute the little white mouse sets forth again refusing to listen to the words of the spider and the worm. He runs with all the strength he can muster and reaches out for the vine. It was strong and secure. He pulls himself up to the lip of the pit and onto the ground. The little mouse collapses on the ground, still clinging to the vine. When he finally stands up, he is greeted by a leaf full of morning dew waiting to refresh him.

The mouse had fallen many times, resisted the dark voices, struggled, and persevered. Ultimately, he had forgiven his tormentors and cried out for help to the Maker of heaven and earth. His reward was experiencing His faithfulness and lovingkindness. Leaving the spider and the worm behind, he gleefully escaped into the beauty of the new day with a thankful heart and eyes wide open.

He shared his experience with everyone he met: "The Lord preserved me and kept me alive, and I am blessed upon the earth. I waited patiently for the Lord; and He inclined unto me and heard my cry. He brought me up out of a horrible pit, out of the miry clay and set my feet upon a rock and established my goings" (Psalm 40:1). "He did not deliver me unto the will of my enemies. He strengthened me upon my bed of languishing" (Psalm 41:2).

CHAPTER 12

IDENTITY

Becoming born again is the most important decision in a person's life. By believing in Jesus and asking Him to be their Savior and Lord the person experiences a miraculous transformation. Instantly their sins are remitted and they become a new creature in Christ Jesus (2 Corinthians 5:17). Remit means to cancel guilt or penalty, to be freed from a punishment or debt (Webster Dictionary). "With the heart man believes unto righteousness and with the mouth confession is made unto salvation" (Romans 10:10).

"For if by one man's offense death reigned (Adam), much more they which receive abundance of grace and the gift of righteousness shall reign in life by one, Jesus Christ" (Romans 5:17).

Righteousness means right standing with God. It is a gift given to us by the Father because of what Jesus did on our behalf. We will never be more righteous than we are the moment we were born again. With the heart we believe and with our mouth we confess Jesus as Savior and Lord. It is the way we receive everything else from God. We believe with our heart and confess with the words of our mouth. We can grow and develop spiritually but we cannot grow in righteousness. Just as a baby is born a human being and he can grow and develop as a child, a teen and an adult but he cannot become more of a human. If a person has blue eyes before they are born again, they will still have blue eyes after their conversion experience because what happens at the new birth is not physical it is spiritual.

Jesus told us in John 3:3 that we must be born again. He also said He is the way, the truth and the life. All roads do not lead to God the Father. Jesus is the only way to the Father. Once we have made the decision to accept Jesus into our hearts Romans 8:17 tells us that we are heirs of God and joint heirs with Jesus Christ. That means whatever belongs to Jesus belongs to us. The Bible, especially the New Testament, details what the inheritance and privileges are for the child of God.

The main benefits are:

- Our sins are completely forgiven and blotted out. They are not covered; they are blotted out (2 Corinthians 5:17).
- The Holy Spirit comes to live in our human spirit and will never leave us (1 John 4:4).
- We become a son/daughter of God and receive an inheritance (1 John 4:4 and Ephesians 1:11).
- All things become possible to us because we have believed in Jesus (Mark 9:23).
- We are able to live an abundant life here on earth (John 10:10).

The sixth chapter of Romans teaches us that Jesus became as we were so that we could become as He is. Jesus became one with us in sin so that we could become one with Him in right standing with the Heavenly Father (righteousness). He became one with us in death so that we could become one with Him in life. He became sick and weak so that we could be healed, healthy and strong.

Isaiah 53 details the punishment he bore so that we could be saved, healed, delivered and made whole. Jesus was not martyred. He willingly gave up His life so that we willingly could choose life with the Father. The same Holy Spirit who raised Jesus from the dead lives in each of us who are born again. The Holy Spirit guides, comforts and teaches us and He will remind us of what Jesus has told us.

Obstacles

Man is a spirit, possesses a soul and lives in a body. When man dies his body dies. His spirit and soul do not die. They are separated from the body and continue to live either in heaven or hell based on the decision made here on this earth regarding Jesus. The real you is spirit. Your spirit should train and direct your soul (mind, will and emotions) and your body. Your old man died and you became a new creation in Christ Jesus. Your spirit man became empowered to influence your mind, which must be renewed by the Word of God and your body must be trained to obey your spirit. We never lose our free will. Just as we are free to accept or reject Jesus, we are free to allow the new nature to dominate our soul and body or to yield to the flesh, the world and the devil.

If we sin (miss the mark) after we have been born again God does not abandon us. We are still His children and He is still our Father. He is with us and loves us. He is against the sin because it is evil and hurts us and can hurt others, but He is not against us. He loves us and wants to help us. There may be a consequence to the sin but the consequence does not change the Father's love. For example, if a man and woman have sex outside of marriage and the women gets pregnant, they can repent of the fornication but the consequence is still there. The child is growing in her womb and they both are responsible to deliver and care for the child. If a man steals and is arrested, he can repent and be forgiven by God but he is still responsible for the consequence of his actions to those he injured and to society. The good news is that there is always hope in God if repentance is sincere. God knows if the person is sincerely sorry and wants to change or if they are only sorry, they got caught. The Father will open his arms wide to accept the one who turns to Him with a sincere heart (Luke 15:20).

The Apostle John, speaking to Christians, wrote that: "If we confess our sins, He is faithful and just to forgive us of our sins, and to cleanse us of all unrighteousness" (1John 1:9). In First John 2:1 He said: "My little children (sons and daughters) these things I write to you, that you not sin. But if you do sin you have an advocate with the Father." Jesus is our advocate (defense attorney) in the courtroom of heaven.

Repentance is not a change in behavior. Change of behavior is a result of a change of heart and mind. Repentance is changing your mind about who you are. If you believe what the word says about who you are your behavior will change and stay changed. If you do not change what you believe about yourself you will soon revert back to the negative behavior. If you fall it is your flesh that has failed. Remember who you are in Christ. Confess the sin and get back up, regain your position as a son/daughter of the king and move forward. This is impossible to do unless you have been transformed by the new birth. But if you are born again, the Holy Spirit can help you change your mind and change your behavior. If He was able to raise Jesus from the dead, He is able to raise you out of sin and restore you.

Being in Christ is what makes you a Christian. Everything Jesus has you have and everything Jesus did you can do. Every curse against your life has been broken because Jesus became a curse for you (Galatians 3:13). All of the blessings or favor you receive, anything good that you do, or any accomplishment are all because of who Jesus is in you so there is no need to boast. He took your sin, sickness, failure, pain, and weakness. All of it was put on Him so you could be complete and entire lacking nothing. That is the great exchange, the grace and mercy of God upon your life. You did not earn it and you don't deserve it but it has become yours because of Jesus. Your part is to believe it, receive it and thank Him for it.

The spiritual nature of man without Christ is a fallen nature. But believers in Christ are not fallen. They have the nature of God inside them. The problem with many Christians is that they are looking in the wrong mirror. They are looking in the natural mirror with all its flaws and limitations or in the rear-view mirror at their past. The only mirror a believer should be looking in is the mirror of the spirit. The mirror of the spirit is the Word of God. What does God say about you? Are you speaking words that agree with what He says about you or are you in agreement with what your past experience or what the enemy is saying about you?

Identity theft is constantly being released against every believer on the planet. Adamantly refuse to let it happen to you. In the spirit realm arrest the thief and expose his lies. Reinforce the truth about who you are in Christ by speaking out the truth.

Just as Satan lied to Eve, he tries to deceive us by attacking our identity as sons and daughters of God. In the wilderness Satan tempted Jesus by saying "if you are the son of God..." Notice he misquoted God. God the Father said, "This is my beloved son". Satan left out the "beloved" part and he does the same with us. Jesus put Satan in his place with the Word of God. He said, "It is written". We will defeat the enemy by speaking out what is written in the scriptures. But in order to do that we have to know what is written in the Bible and rightly divide the word of God knowing that we are no longer wretched sinners we are now beloved children who have been forgiven and promised an inheritance.

Jesus came to allow us to experience Zoe life. What does Zoe life look like? It looks like Adam and Eve before the fall; intimate relationship with God the Father, fellowship with one another, and harmony with creation. It looks like peace and joy as our spirit, soul and body come into agreement with God's love for us as his children made in his image and filled with his spirit. The fruit of the Spirit is given to every believer at the point of salvation. The fruit is part of our new nature and it is the very heart of God. Jesus came to reveal the Father to mankind.

God does not have love He is love. He does not have peace, He is peace. He does not have faithfulness, He is faithfulness, joy, gentleness, etc. As we yield to the fruit of the spirit in us, we will bear good fruit. Galatians 5:16 tells us that: "those who walk and live in the Spirit (who are responsive and controlled by the Holy Spirit) will not fulfill the lust of the flesh." 2 Peter 1:10 says: "those who walk in the Spirit will never fall."

We walk in the Spirit by staying in fellowship with the Lord Jesus. Keeping our eyes on Him is the way we obey His directive to stay connected to the vine. In John 15:4-8 and John 14:7 Jesus said "If you have seen Me you have seen the Father." The goal is complete union with Jesus and He would never tell us to do something we could not accomplish. The good news is that we are not doing it in our own strength. If we try to become like Jesus by our own willpower we will utterly fail. We do it with the help of the wonderful Holy Spirit who is teaching us, guiding us and encouraging us every step of the way.

Ask Holy Spirit to show you who you really are and how to be the person God intended you to be. Study the scriptures that use the phrase "in Christ", "in Him", "in whom" or "through whom". Start with the first three chapters of the book of Ephesians and meditate on who He says you are. "You shall know the truth and the truth shall set you free" (John 8:32).

CHAPTER 13

BITTER ROOT

(Ray's story)

He awakened with heaviness of soul. The only thing he could relate it to was a hangover, but he had not been drinking. His life seems to be one blur after another of unfulfilled dreams and desires. He worked hard but he never flourished on any job. His efforts were not enough and the money was never enough. Now his marriage was in trouble and he was desperate for answers. He felt trapped. His wife did not say the words but he could hear them all the same, "Ray, you are not enough." He knew he had never been enough.

The ceiling over his life seemed to come closer with each passing year. His inability to connect with his emotions or to articulate kept him an arm's length from success, both on his job and in his marriage. No matter how hard he worked and how responsible he was he was always passed over for promotion and each time he was unable to speak up and ask for what he felt he deserved.

Ray loved his wife but never felt adequate to meet her needs. They had become like strangers, living in the same house but never together. Sleeping in the same bed and having sex but with no true intimacy. He knew she loved him but she was lonely and wanted to connect to him but he could not connect to himself so how could he help her. She wanted to know him at a deep level, with her heart, with her emotions, but he was like a stone in those areas. She of course interpreted that to mean that she was unattractive and insignificant, but that was a lie. He complimented her and encouraged her but nothing seemed to satisfy her desire to be one with him in more than a superficial way.

Therapy had not helped. They seemed to go in circles that never reaped an answer or pose any valid solution. He came away from each session feeling like more of a failure than when he started. In desperation he agreed when his wife asked him to meet with a Christian minister at their church for prayer. Perhaps God would have mercy on him and set him free, if not, at least he would know he had done all he could do to save his marriage.

After a short opening prayer, the minister asked him if he was in agreement to allowing the Holy Spirit to show him the root of the problem. He agreed. He was then directed to focus his attention on Jesus and wait silently until the Holy Spirit brought him a memory or spoke something to his heart. That quiet time was uncomfortable but he honestly tried to focus on Jesus. Suddenly he saw a black square in his mind's eye.

He saw himself as a six-year old boy standing on a black square tile. When asked what that meant to him with no emotion, he explained that it was the kitchen floor of the house in Peru where he had grown up. The minister was patient as it took what seemed like an eternity before he spoke again. Finally, he proceeded to relay that his mother cleaned and polished that floor like a mirror. She was a perfectionist and desired him to be perfect as well. When he drew her wrath at what she perceived to be the slightest infraction she would force him to stand on that one black tile.

As he grew older the sessions on the black tile started getting longer. Sometimes the sun would set before he could leave the tile and if he would wet his pants in the process of waiting, she would beat him for having soiled her floor. Each time she punished him his heart become harder. The more she tried to break his will the firmer he became in his resolve to resist her. Soon he became the object of her wrath with little or no provocation. It no longer was about any specific infraction on his part but rather a tug of war between them for control. He resolved that she could make him stand on that black tile but she could never make him cry. Even when she beat him with a wooden spoon he refused to cry. He determined she would never control his emotions even if she could control his body by her strength. Although he had left Peru and his mother many years ago, he was still under the control of her tyranny. He could still hear her words echoing in his mind "You are such a disappointment to this family. You can't do anything right and you are a very bad boy."

His identity and value had been marred and his emotions shut down. The words she cursed him with had place a ceiling over him and he had long ago been taught that he would never be able to please a woman. His mother had been abusive and controlling but his volitional decision to not cry shut down his emotions. That vow against her was now exacting a great price in his marriage. It was the only way a small boy could fight back but he had made a bitter root judgment against his mother and the inner vow was now costing him his life. Unable to feel pain he also was unable to feel anything else. What she had done to him was a terrible abuse of power and had severely damaged his self-image, but he was not six years old now.

As an adult the same exercise of his will that had judged her and made a vow against her could release him from her control and her curses. The way out of this trap for him was to forgive her and give the violation to God for judgment. In doing so he would surrender his demand to be loved by her and take back his power to love, expecting nothing in return. He could then take back the parts cut off from him as a child by rejection and abuse and renounce the vows he had made so that he could actually risk relationship with others.

Ray forgave his mother and broke ungodly soul ties with her. As an act of his will he blessed her but refused to accept anything ungodly from her. He came out of agreement with the lies she had spoken about him and forgave himself for believing them. He asked the Lord to forgive him for hating her and making vows against her. He asked his wife to forgive him for having transferred those vows to her and withholding himself from her emotionally. He confessed insecurity, fear and self-hatred. He asked the Lord to break down the fortress and teach him how to trust others. He renounced the vows he had made to withhold his emotions and asked the Lord to give him grace to feel and have balanced emotions.

The prayer minister prayed and asked the Holy Spirit to break the demonic strongholds in his life and to cleanse him of all the negative imprints, heal his wounded soul and fill him with hope. As a prophetic act Ray stood up and took a step off that black square and as an act of his will, he declared that he refused to ever stand on it again. Ray was free to be the person God created him to be. The love of his wife had helped him seek help from the Holy Spirit and it would be her continued love that would help him grow and flourish in his newfound freedom.

Control

Control at the core is a spirit that has run rampant since the day in the Garden of Eden when Adam and Eve yielded to the manipulation, deceit and control of Satan. The same jealous, hateful throne seeking spirit is at work through people today.

Divine order in the home, the church and in a nation is based on the law of love. Divine order must first seek relationship with God, and then with others. Only then can decisions be made that are mutually beneficial. God never intended for men or women to have dominion over each other, their children or others. The enemy has twisted and perverted control. Instead of controlling ourselves he has tricked us into controlling others by deceiving us into believing that it will make us safer or more powerful. He has tricked us into believing that the end justifies the means because by exerting control over others we are establishing order in the home, on the job or in the church. Proverbs 29:11 teaches us that a wise man keeps himself under control. Therefore, self-control is the only control we are to be exercising.

Abuse under the banner of authority (husband, parent, pastor, teacher, coach) is still abuse. Jesus does not want his people abused nor for them to submit to abuse. The root system of control and manipulation is held in place through the paralysis of fear. The motive of everything Jesus did was love and he has not changed. He said he would send the Holy Spirit to help us, comfort us and lead us not dominate or control us. The key issue in the process of restoration of our souls to health and freedom is to know whose control we are yielding to. Walking in the Spirit means being yielded to the Holy Spirit and following the law of love. Have you entrusted yourself to the control of the Holy Spirit or are you under the control of someone else?

Control is always rooted in fear. People rooted in fear respond to life by trying to control others or circumstances instead of trusting in God's love and provision. Satan wants to control your ability to connect with God and your power to walk in authority on this earth. Jesus came to set you free from his control. Yielding to the work of the Holy Spirit is the first step to freedom in Christ. Our motive for yielding to the work of the Holy Spirit must be that we may be healed and free to love God more deeply, trust him more completely and know Him more intimately.

If you are operating in control, he wants you free. If you are under the control of another, He wants you free. Jesus entrusted Himself to His Heavenly Father. Entrust yourself to the Heavenly Father and He will heal and deliver you so that you can learn to walk in the authority you have been given.

Judgments and Vows

The words used in expressing a judgment, vow or curse are in and of themselves neutral. However, the words we use are empowered by either God or Satan, based on our intent or invitation. Just as words are empowered to hold us in bondage (judgments, vows, curses) so also words can be empowered to release us from bondage (repenting, forgiving, renouncing and blessing).

The dynamic of a bitter root judgment is that Satan takes the laws of God and uses them against us. Our judgments against parents or authority figures become a source of demonic power to bring about in our lives the very things we judged against others (Matt. 7:1-2).

Ask the Holy Spirit to surface any judgments, vows or curses made against a parent or authority figure. Once discovered, bitter root judgments are renounced one at a time in the name of the Lord Jesus Christ. This severs them and breaks their power in the spirit realm. You will still have to exercise choice of will to change behaviors and attitudes, but the legal right of the demonic bondage is broken.

The process is the same as it was for Ray. It starts with a decision to come to the Holy Spirit for help.

- Ask the Holy Spirit to show you the core/root of the problem.
- What was done to you? How did you react to it?
- As an act of your will choose to forgive others and ask for forgiveness for your reaction to what happened as a result (Luke 17:3-4 and Matt 6:14).
- Break ungodly soul ties. (Judges 20:11, 1Sam.18:1, Col. 2:2, 2:19)
- Surrender you demands to the Lord and ask for the healing of your soul (Eph. 3:16-17).
- Renounce any vows you have made and confess and repent of lies you have believed (Eph. 4:17-24).

- Destroy the fortresses by surrendering them to Jesus and ask the Holy Spirit to break demonic holds (Cor. 10:3-5).
- Allow Jesus to wash you and take your pain and shame (Jeremiah 2:22).
- Receive His forgiveness and His healing.

Get off whatever black tile you have been standing on. Jesus came to set you free. His desire is that you be healed and become all that you were created to be. His love and power are more than enough to make you the person He intended you to be.

CHAPTER 14

RED BRICK WALL

(Amber's story)

While ministering at a conference in Anaheim, California a young woman from Arizona asked for prayer. All her joints were visibly swollen and painful. Amber was struggling with doing normal daily activities and nothing the medical community offered had been effective in reducing the inflammation.

During prayer the Lord showed me in the spirit a red brick wall with one brick missing in the center. Light was shining through the one missing brick. The Holy Spirit revealed that the red brick wall represented anger. When asked if she was angry with anyone her immediate reply was that she was angry with her father. She reported that her father had been extremely verbally and physically abusive to her and her mother and that she had left home at an early age to escape his abuse. She felt that she had a legitimate right to be angry and had consequently not forgiven him. The Holy Spirit revealed that her anger was internalized and now manifesting in her body as inflammation.

We ministered to her what Jesus said about forgiving others. We explained that to forgive someone does not mean that we negate what the person has done. We obey the directive of scripture by releasing the person, what they have done and the debt owed to us to the Lord. It was a difficult decision for her. She had used her anger in an effort to protect herself and now was faced with trusting the Holy Spirit to protect her. She finally yielded to the Word of God and forgave her father releasing him to the Lord and repented for her anger, bitterness and fear. At that moment the Lord set Amber free of the pain and resentment. The brick wall had been built over many years one brick at a time but in an instant, it was demolished and the light of God's grace flooded her soul. Her swollen joints returned to normal before our eyes and within minutes she was pain free. Both her soul and her body were healed by the power of the Holy Spirit once she chose to forgive.

God's grace was always available to Amber but she had to choose to be obedient to the Word of God before that grace could flow to her. Only by her obedience was she able to get realigned with God's provision, which included healing and deliverance. Her capacity to receive had been blocked by the wall of anger.

Repentance is humbly admitting that we are wrong. Asking for forgiveness and forgiving others is humbling. The primary reason for confession is for our benefit. When we confess our sins, we come into agreement with God that what we did or failed to do was in rebellion against his law of love. God wants us restored to mercy and grace by our choice to let go of rebellion and stubbornness, and submit to humility and obedience.

We each have the right to choose. Satan can't cross our will. If we choose not to be afraid or not to lie or not to be offended no one and nothing can force us to do it. Our power is in choosing to exercise our personal will over and against the will of rebellion. As we read the Bible and see what the will of the Lord is, we can decree and declare what we choose. For example, we can read 1 Peter 5:5 and say "I choose to be clothed with humility. It is against my will to be proud. I choose to receive the grace of God by being humble. It is against my will to be stubborn. I choose to admit when I am wrong and I choose to forgive others when they wrong me and ask for forgiveness when I have wronged others."

The greatest gift we have each received is the gift of life which is accompanied by the gift of choice. Choice is a spiritual law and is what sets us apart from the rest of creation. We have the opportunity to choose life or death. When an opportunity or situation presents its self, we have the option to exercise our free will and that option is processed through our soul (mind, will and emotions). Day by day and moment by moment we choose to obey or disobey God's directive (Joshua 24:15). God has plans for us and Satan has plans for us. We get to choose which plan we will align with. Jesus is the way to abundant life. All other ways lead to death, loss or destruction (John 14:6 & John 10:10).

Rebellion is rooted in fear and if not dealt with will result in lawlessness. Thinking that we have a right to sit in judgment of those in authority over us is the same sin that Lucifer committed against God. This includes criticism of ministers, government, parents, employers etc. Submitting to authority and choosing to believe that God will protect us will result in our being blessed and all will go well with us. Amber was right in protecting herself from her father's abuse. But she was not right in harboring un-forgiveness and anger against him.

1 Samuel 15:23 teaches us that rebellion is as the sin of witchcraft. Witchcraft is the use of sorcery or magic, communication with demons or with familiar spirits, a fascination with enchantment. Divination is seeking power or knowledge from any spirit source other than the Holy Spirit. God hates divination because it leads people to seek satanic intelligence for guidance in their lives instead of trusting Him and His word. Critical attitudes and rejection are a subtle form of control. The underlying motive is to threaten and manipulate. All manipulative control is rebellion. Manipulation, domination and control are the tools of witchcraft and it is not surprising, therefore, that the victim can be demonized as a result.

"I have called you back from the ends of the earth so you can serve Me. For I have chosen you and will not throw you away (Isaiah 41:9)." It is God's will that none should perish but that all come to repentance. Rebellion is an issue of self-will, which has become embedded in the heart. Pray for a softening of the heart, for a breaking of self will. Ask that all ground given over to unclean spirits through rebellion be cancelled and covered by the blood of Jesus.

As the young lady with the wall of anger your walls can be torn down in a moment. The choice is yours. Choose obedience - choose forgiveness.

CHAPTER 15

ARROW OF OFFENSE

(Mark's story)

Every church he had been involved with had slowly inched him off the platform. Mark was a gifted musician yet he was unable to maintain his position. With each rejection he had taken offense and now he was on the brink of spiritual disaster. He had one foot in the church and one foot in the world. He had repented many times of complaining and murmuring against pastors and leaders, only to return again to drink of the same bitter water. Year after year offense had woven its way into the fabric of his soul.

The alligator has a huge smile but a mouth full of sharp teeth and is a representation of how critical words tear and consume others. Had he contained his complaints or taken them directly to the offender he might have been less vulnerable, but he criticized openly and brought his contention to others in an effort to justify himself. His words were released like razors and the offense enticed him to swallow the bait every time. His continual murmuring against authority opened a trap door, which hurled him headlong into a pit of despair. He was now so disillusioned that he felt death would be a relief from the torment of constant rejection. Rightly does the scripture admonish us not be a mocker or a scorner that we not be consumed.

As a young man he had enjoyed the company of other musicians and pressed hard to make a place for himself among his peers only to have a leader ask him to step down. Miscarriage after miscarriage hardened his heart and in time affected his music. What had started as vision and passion to use his musical ability to worship God had become shipwrecked. Most recently he had prostituted his gift playing in a nightclub. By day he taught music and by night he escaped into the numbness of alcohol. His soul was in torment as he discarded the love for the things of God he had once embraced for the lie he now lived.

His father had been an attorney and expected his son to follow suit. There was no room for creativity in his analytical, dogmatic world of law. He was rigid about his son's career path and failed to consider his heart in the matter. When his son refused the role assigned him, the demand for compliance escalated and the battle of wills began. They arm-wrestled for control and grew farther and farther apart with each passing year. Mark was fourteen when resistance gave birth to rebellion. He began to escape into the hills on his bike traveling into the arms of nature. Hours of hiking and playing his flute or guitar under the canopy of trees was a welcomed distraction. Anything was better than being home with his browbeating father who verbalized his hot displeasure at every opportunity. "You are a nobody going nowhere" were the words that echoed in his ears as he ran out the door.

Over time the rejection Mark had experienced from his father showed up in teachers, employers and pastors alike. With each new disappointment he withdrew to lick his wounds as he recounted the litany of complaints against those in authority. With each perceived injustice the stumbling block of offense grew and now had become a great arrow in his heart.

The cycle was predictable. He would vent his rage in self-righteous condemnation, his words poisoning anyone who would listen. Self-pity would then lead him to a dark pit of depression where he would give himself over to hatred as he drowned himself in alcohol. In years past his rage had been against others but recently it had turned inward. Now when he entered that pit, he slept with hopelessness and entertained a dark desire to die. That arrow of offense was threatening to kill him with its poison. When Mark awakened from his stupor he would be flooded with guilt and shame.

Many had prayed with him and many more had prayed for him, yet he remained locked in the cycle of bitter destruction. His words shot bullets at those whom he perceived to be ruining his life as well as against those who failed to agree with him. Was God impotent and prayers not fervent enough to break his chains? Or had his arrow of offense included God the Father for assigning him an oppressive parent and giving men authority over him? Was God deaf or was it that this young man had shut the door to the very one that could deliver him.

In Genesis 15:1-2 we are told that God revealed Himself to Abram in a vision saying, "Do not fear, Abram, I am a shield to you; your reward shall be very great." And Abram answered and said, "O Lord God, what will you give me, since I am childless?" God went on to promise him an heir and a great multitude as his inheritance.

The name that Abram addressed God by in this passage is translated in the Hebrew as Jehovah Adoni, meaning my Lord, Master and Owner. He acknowledged God's right as creator of the universe to own him and everything that was his. He also came to know Him as the God who would deliver him from his enemies, comfort him, and richly bless him. But first he acknowledged him as master; a master who knew the best path for him and who was faithful to his promises.

As with the leper who fell at the feet of Jesus and asked to be made clean Mark had to choose to humble himself and acknowledge God as his Lord if he was to be set free of his oppression. Before Mark could know God as His healer and deliver, he had to know him as Lord and Master in practice not only in principle. In Luke 6:46 Jesus asked, "Why do you call me Lord, Lord and do not do what I say?"

What are the clear directives we have from our Creator? First of all, to love God the Father, Adoni, with all our heart, mind, soul, and strength and to love others as we love ourselves. Jesus said that this is the great commandment. Every other directive in scripture is given to enforce this commandment. To forgive as we have been forgiven and to do it at all times and in all situations; to bless even those who curse us; to forsake judging and murmuring against others, including God. We are to do justly, to love mercy, and walk humbly with our God (Micha 6:8).

Real wrongs had been committed against Mark. His father had not nurtured him nor had he represented God well by controlling and verbally abusing him. Others in positions of authority had also discounted him and passed him over. They had not followed the great commandment to love him. But the release for Mark was not in vindication and revenge but rather in his response to those who had offended him. The bitter root judgment he had made against his father had been transferred to every other authority figure and the arm wrestle for control had never ended. The arrow of offense was burning hot with the poison of rage as he clutched it to his heart. He had a clear choice to make. Hold on to offense and continue in his torment until he self-destructed or acknowledge Jehovah Adoni and be obedient to His commandment. Of course, that would mean letting go of his longtime friends, self-pity being the closest and unforgiveness, rebellion, anger and resentment running close behind. Self-pity sat on his shoulder like a scorpion. A pinch from that vice grip would be just enough pain to set the downward cycle into motion once again. God will not deliver us from our friends. Mark alone could decide to evict his ungodly companions. He had set his will to rebel against his father when he was a teenager, what would he choose now? He had managed to do the minimum at school and had gone as far from academia as he could. But had he won the battle with his father only to lose the war over his soul?

Is there an arrow of offense that you are holding onto? That mirror which reflects every wrong that has been committed against you must be shattered if you are to be free. Unforgiveness carries a price tag you cannot afford to pay. Choosing to acknowledge your Creator as Adoni and submitting to His wisdom of how you are to respond to those who have hurt you is the only way to destroy both the arrow and the mirror. Blessing you will be blessed and forgiving you will be forgiven. I reiterate, forgiveness does not change the debt owed you by those who have hurt you. You are merely giving up your right to vengeance and allowing God to collect the debt. The only way for any of us to escape the death trap jaws of the alligator is to stop the words we release in judgment against others and to forgive the offense as we ourselves have been forgiven.

Choose to do the right thing, the hard thing, immediately. Waiting only delays the decision. It does not get easier because you wait. Denial will only prolong the hard choice and compounds the emotional pain.

CHAPTER 16

TANDEM BIKE

(Tina's story)

"I'm just a nervous wreck. I don't know how I got into this mess. Three years ago, I was debt free and now I have $32,000 in credit card debt on top of the car payment. I'm working two jobs but I am not able to make the payments anymore. There really isn't anything I can do about it. I guess I will have to file bankruptcy. I'm trying hard not to be myself because I make a mess of everything, but I'm having trouble knowing how to be someone else. I can't eat or sleep. I just want to be home with my mom again."

Truth, not bankruptcy, was the only thing that could rescue Tina. Without truth she would only repeat the cycle in a few short years. She had to be honest and face what had brought her to this crisis. Living in the past is a trap door with no key.

However, we may want to visit the past when it is affecting our present in order to pull out the bad roots and weeds that are choking and stifling our growth.

As a child Tina always wanted to be sick so she could stay home with her mom. They got along so well, laughing and playing together. They made a pact against dad and loved to play trick on him. They buried or hid things just to drive him crazy. He worked hard and was always tired; no fun, no affection, just the boss who held the purse strings.

His wife rejected him emotionally and taught her daughter to do the same. He tried to connect with Tina but mom always blocked his efforts and poisoned her mind against him.

When Tina was seven, she stole two silver dollars and gave them to the neighborhood boys. She was trying to buy their friendship but it did not work. They took her money and then tormented her with their words. At age eleven she escaped into soap operas with her mom and started reading romance novels. She kissed all the boys in her class and they loved it. She finally found something that interested boys and kept their attention. They called her a tease and she loved it.

Just after her eleventh birthday her world changed and she slid into a deep depression. She explained: "I'll never forgive my dad for losing his job and selling our house. Everything changed and it's all his fault. On top of having to move, change schools and mom going to work I started my period and it grossed me out. I wanted to stay a child and be home or just die because it was all too hard. Three summers later we went on a trip to Sequoia and I almost drowned in the river. It was scary and exciting all at the same time. I almost drowned but was rescued by a strong young man named Nick who jumped in and pulled me to safety."

After that trip Tina suffered one illness after another: chronic mono, Epstein Bar, chronic fatigue and headaches. Now she was sick not to be home with mom but to be on prescription drugs that rescued her from pain and allowed her to avoid life.

She was defensive one moment and aggressive the next. Living in denial and then wanting to escape. It was all so confusing and exhausting. The child and adult were at war. What started out as a game with mom developed into a pattern of escape and a mindset confused about the role of men in her life. How could she know who she was when everything was filtered through the eyes of her mother? Angry female, victim, tease, creating situations so that she might be rescued and most damaging of all being sick and crying out for pain relief resulting in addiction. She was co-dependent with her mom. They were symbiotic spirits feeding off of each other. The love hate battle with her dad was confusing to her and to every man she met. She self-sabotaged in an effort to be rescued. She had never learned that genuine healthy relationships are reciprocal but not dependent. Like a wave being tossed in a never-ending storm of conflicting emotions she was double-minded on steroids.

"Oh, that I had wings like a dove; for then I would fly away and be at rest. Then I would wander far off and remain in the wilderness. I would escape from the windy storm" (Psalm 55:6).

Tina had recently heard the good news of Jesus and embraced Him as her ultimate rescuer. Her spirit was genuinely born again and she was desperate to be free of the debt and prescription drugs. She turned to Him for healing of her body but the root of her problem was in her soul. Her spirit was reborn by her conversion experience but her mind, will and emotions were severely damaged and the fruit of that damage was manifesting in her physical body.

Her healing started with a sincere choice to face the truth. One by one the lies were exposed and she looked at them square in the face. Choosing to yield her will to the truth of the Word of God inched her forward day by day. She chose to forgive her father for his absence and lack of connection. She chose to forgive her mother for keeping her a dependent child and poisoning her against her father. She broke ungodly soul ties with her mom and asked the Lord to heal her mind of all the wrong things she had learned from her. The hardest thing for her to do was to allow the little girl to rest and decide to grow up. She slowly forgave herself for every poor choice she had made and all the excuses she had fashioned to remain a victim who needed to be rescued.

Tina got the breakthrough the day she admitted that her mind was split, confused and troubled because she was so full of herself. The only remedy was to focus on the truth. She started to meditate on what God had to say and that silenced the voices in her crying out for attention. She learned to be still and listen to the voice of the Holy Spirit and not all the madness. She stopped making excuses for the compulsive spending and the need for drugs. She negotiated with her creditors and started to pay down the debt one paycheck at a time. She was honest about how she had gotten into the mess and made a concrete budget plan to get out of the maze.

"I knew I could not do it before I even started but Jesus said He would help me so that changed everything. I was not doing anything by my own effort, we were doing it together. It was like riding a tandem bike. Holy Spirit was in front taking the load and leading the way. I had to peddle and allow Him to lead me. We did it together. I was never alone and it was not impossible to change or to be free. I had hope!"

From that point forward Tina trained herself to take every thought captive. Trying to understand where it came from was not the point. The critical point was to do something about it. Fighting the negative thoughts with words of life she exchanged each lie with truth. She accepted Jesus as her superhero. He came to rescue her but she had to allow Him to do it. She had to yield to Him and focus on Him, believe that He loved her and that He would give her all the grace she needed to do the right thing, the hard thing.

It took six years for Tina to pay off the debt and find out who she really was, but she did it. She changed one day at a time, one choice at a time and one truth at a time. The peace came as she renewed her mind with the scriptures. The joy came as she abandoned her victim mentality and the need to escape or be rescued. She stumbled a few times along the way, but each time she had the courage to get back on the tandem bike and keep peddling. With each new start she became stronger and more determined. Truly old thing passed away and all things were made new in her life.

"Blessed be the Lord who has not given me as prey to their teeth. My soul has escaped as a bird out of a trap; the trap is broken and I have escaped. My help is in the Name of the Lord who made heaven and earth." Psalm 124:16-17 became her life verse.

CHAPTER 17

HANDCUFFS

(Ben's story)

He sat slumped in his chair; a cup almost tipped over in his long bony fingers. Despite the weight loss Ben was still a large man at 6'4". Although drugs had him in a semi-stupor his eyes followed the conversation and his head turned ever so slightly at the mention of his name. His words were a raspy whisper that faded as quickly as they were released. Here sat a man reduced to a mere shadow of his former self. When we had first met five years earlier, he was full of energy and animated as he spoke, a business owner and sales magnet full of himself and sure that nothing could daunt him.

As a young man his size served him well as he maneuvered through the tough neighborhoods of Brooklyn. He could hold his own in any street fight and talked his way in and out of situations with ease. Abandoned by his father at four he learned how to be a man from those who ruled the streets. Alcohol became his escape from the pain of victimization and the abuse he encountered in that process.

He was a master at telling people what they wanted to hear and soon realized his mouth could serve him better than his fists. Financial success followed his gift of gab and eventually he opened his own business. Unfortunately, alcohol and gambling kept him struggling despite his flourishing business. He was double minded, slick and stylish businessman and a rough abusive street kid all wrapped into one.

When I met Ben, he was desperate to save his marriage to the woman who kept his business afloat. He turned to God for help. His marriage was restored but now, three years later, he found himself in the fight of his life and neither his mouth nor his fists could win this battle.

Tattoos on his forehead, chin and temples marked a perfect cross on his long-drawn face. Five rounds of radiation to his head had drained him of every ounce of energy. In the years since he and his wife had accepted Jesus Christ as their Savior, they had made some strides in spiritual growth but their business and the financial demands kept them from the renewal of the mind that only comes from total emersion in the Word of God.

He would get prayer and rebound but was unable to hold onto ground gained because of doubt and unbelief. Fear was running rampant in both of them and no amount of prayer or counsel convinced them to believe God's word for his healing over the medical reports. Both his and her words canceled out all the progress and prayers released on his behalf.

Ben mistakenly believed God had put this sickness on him so he had no faith to believe God would remove it. He had a big tab of gambling debt and a bigger list of wrongs against himself. He was plagued with guilt and refused to forgive himself. Years of verbal abuse on his part had severely damaged his wife and they both struggled with deep roots of bitterness and unresolved issues. Abandonment and rejection by his father and abuse from the men in his life had left him angry and hardened. In his lifetime he had released many evil words against others and now he was throwing stones at himself. He believed he deserved what he was now experiencing because of his past. He had a choice just as the women caught in adultery did. Jesus said to her "Women, where are your accusers, has no man condemned you? Neither do I condemn you. Go and sin no more" (John 8:11).

Ben did deserve to be punished for all he had done against others, himself and his Creator. But the greater truth was that Jesus had taken the punishment he deserved so that he could go free. His body was destroying itself in agreement with self-condemnation. He refused to embrace the love of his Heavenly Father. Christ having died to save him from eternal damnation was as far as his faith could go. All of it was cleansed by the blood of Jesus and forgiven by the Heavenly Father the very day Ben had accepted Jesus as his personal savior but he refused to believe it. Cancer did not destroy Ben's health. His self-hatred and self-condemnation did. Self-condemnation is a ruthless killer. It is twisted thinking which keeps you in handcuffs. Psalm 118:18 reads: "The Lord corrects severally but He does not give us over to death." Satan comes to kill, steal and destroy not God. (John 10:10)

When God told the children of Israel to go in and take the promised land, He gave them two instructions. First, they were to dispose of the enemies that were in the land and secondly, they were to tear down their images. Ben had demonic enemies and demonic images of himself. Deep seeded self-hatred drove him to slow painful self-destruction. The lie he embraced as a child was that he was disposable and existed only to be used and abused by others. The truth was that he was of great value and beloved of God. But the word of God did not prosper him because it was not mixed with faith.

On the day of Pentecost Peter was being used by God powerfully to preach and minister, turning the hearts of the people to repentance and faith in Jesus Christ. We read in the book of Acts that Peter was so anointed of God that even his shadow brought healing to the sick. This same Peter had only days before been at the lowest point in his life. He wept bitterly in remorse and repentance because he had denied that he even knew Jesus. Sin had knocked Peter down but he got back up. The mercy of God had brought him to repentance. But in order to get back up he had to do one thing. He had to receive the forgiveness of the Father. His ability to receive that forgiveness allowed him to get back on his feet.

Unlike Peter, Judas did not accept God's forgiveness. In Matthew 17:1-5 we read that Judas repented to the high priest and elders. He acknowledged to them that he had sinned and betrayed an innocent man. But when those men refused him instead of turning to God to receive mercy he despaired and went out and hanged himself. Like Peter Judas knew he had done wrong and felt remorse. But he turned to men for help instead of to God. Picture the two men flat on the ground beaten and weak, totally condemned. God speaks to them both and says "You are forgiven, now get up." One believes in his heart that what God has said to him is true and the other does not. He dies there on the ground in abject poverty of soul eaten away by condemnation.

Self-condemnation is alignment with Satan. It will keep you in handcuffs and behind bars all the days of your life. You can't earn your forgiveness by punishing yourself, making promises to change or by doing good works and community service. There is nothing you can do because you are in fact guilty. However, when you step to the right side of the courtroom and come under the protection of the blood of Jesus you receive the grace of God by faith to be forgiven and to forgive yourself. It is the blood of Jesus that cleanses you from all sin, not your good works.

Psalm 120:3-4 reads: "If the Lord should mark iniquities, none would be able to stand?" If God kept account and treated us according to our sins, none of us would have a chance. But there is forgiveness with Him. Sin consciousness and self-condemnation are hooked to a religious spirit. That religious spirit wants to keep you in jail or keep you on a work detail for your entire life. It was for freedom that Christ set you free. Do not quit and do not keep yourself in jail. Repent (turn around) quickly and receive your freedom immediately. Forgiving yourself is the key that will open the handcuffs. Choose to get up by receiving the mercy and grace of God.

As long as you are on the floor you are looking at the sin. When you get up you are electing to believe the Word of the Lord. By faith you accept His forgiveness and choose life. If you admit you did wrong God will forgive you. It is written that if we confess our sins, He is faithful and just to forgive us and cleanse us of all unrighteousness (1 John 1:9). If you have to cry over your sin for a week, be depressed and tell yourself what a worm you are you are in fact saying to Jesus that what He did was not enough and that you have to beat yourself up in order to be forgiven. How prideful is that? It is saying to God, "I do not believe You when You tell me that there is no condemnation to me because I am in Christ Jesus or that what Jesus did was sufficient". This kind of thinking is bondage. Each day we must choose to forgive ourselves and live. Choose to do it quickly and completely. Take off the handcuffs. Be grace conscious and not sin conscious. Honor the One who paid the price for your sin by forgiving yourself. He is worthy of the honor.

CHAPTER 18

CEMENTED THINKING

(Diana's story)

Before me sat a thin stylish woman with a devoted husband and grown children who cherished her. She was successful in her career and made time to reach out and help others. Yet, despite all these blessings, she had lost her ability to connect with the Lord. She reported that she was in a place of dryness in her relationship with God. "I see myself on the bank of a river. Jesus is standing on the opposite shore. I can see Him but I can't get to Him. I am desperate for the relationship I once enjoyed with Him. I can't seem to connect anymore." We prayed asking the Holy Spirit to reveal to her what was blocking her from the intimacy she longed for.

Prompted by the Holy Spirit I asked Diana when she first became aware of the distancing. "It was about the time my mom died six months ago," was her reply. Her mother had been in a critical comatose condition for three weeks. She and her brother had faithfully sat at her bedside throughout those long weeks. On Christmas Eve she decided to fly home to be with her husband and children for a few days. The day after leaving her mother died. Regret flooded her soul. Not one family member blamed her for leaving, yet she had been struggling for many months. She reported having forgiven herself for making that decision yet the level of emotional pain connected to the memory made it clear that there was still an arrow in her heart. Suddenly she broke into tears saying repeatedly, "I am such a selfish person. All I care about is myself. I always choose what is convenient to me." Allowing her time to cry and recompose herself I gently asked her, "Did you ever leave your mother before?" She nodded her head and slowly the story unfolded.

Diana had grown up with years of family turmoil with an alcoholic father and an angry mother. At age eighteen she left home despite her mother's obvious need for help. Her decision had not been made in haste or without struggle but she was desperate to bring peace and order to her life. At that juncture in her life the cycle of blameful thoughts had been established which were rooted in the lie that she was guilty of being selfish. This lie along with the anguish of her decision had torn her soul and bruised her self-image. She had long ago forgiven her father for his drinking and her mother of her anger but she failed to truly release the one caught in the middle of their drama. To understand the bondage, she had to see the parallel between the two events and the lie that was tying them together. In His mercy the Holy Spirit had surfaced the pain in order to heal her wounded soul and set her free.

Year after year the accuser had whispered in her ear and she had made decisive efforts to disprove his accusations. Those who were close to her would report that she was a giving and kind woman. But the harder she demonstrated works of mercy the louder the lie shouted at her that she was selfish. Now she was able to see how contrary to the truth her self-condemnation was. She repented for believing the lie and for aligning herself with the accuser. She asked the Holy Spirit to wash her in His unconditional acceptance and heal the tear in her soul. No longer would she be in bondage to the lie that she was a selfish person.

Self-condemnation is a judgment we hold against ourselves. They can be judgments we ourselves have made or judgments spoken by others against us that we have accepted as true. Embracing accusations against ourselves we put into motion destructive thought patterns that reinforce those lies. The words we say or think against ourselves are keys, which reveal the lies we have believed. Over time the lies become cemented thinking.

The only way out is to bring truth to bear against the lies. Asking the Holy Spirit to bring His light to the darkness of our thoughts will open a door for healing to begin. Evicting self-condemnation includes eviction of the bondage and torment connected to it, such as hopelessness, self-hatred, anger and depression.

Graffiti on a car can't be washed off. The only remedy is to strip the finish down to the bare metal and repaint the car. The same is true with lies. Cutting emotional pain is an alarm that must not be ignored. Just as the rust eats away metal so the lie of condemnation causes a cancer within that eats away at our self-worth. The lie that Diana was selfish was like a tattoo on her soul. No matter how she tried to prove it wrong it was branded on her because she had judged herself. She had been carrying false responsibility for her parents from a very young age. The Bible does say to honor your father and mother. It does not say for a child or a teenager to carry them. The admonition to carry one another's burdens was given to adults not children. It was enough for Diana at eighteen to carry her own load. She was right to clarify the relationships and responsibilities.

God designed our draw to relationship. It causes us to invest time and energy in working things out with others. But trust must be at the core in order for the relationship to be safe. Without trust the relationship will stop working. If you value yourself you will protect yourself. That is what the eighteen-year-old was doing and there was no condemnation to her for choosing to leave the toxic situation. But in doing so she believed a lie and judged herself. Matthew 7:12 reads: Judge not, that you not be judged. For with what judgment you judge you shall be judged, and with the measure you measure, it shall be measured to you again. Have we focused on applying this admonition toward our relationship to others and failed to apply it toward ourselves?

Ask the Holy Spirit to expose any judgments you are holding against yourself and to expose any lies you have believed. Shake off the viper that has put guilt and false responsibility on you. Ask Holy Spirit to use a jackhammer to that cemented thinking and dismantle the wall of self-condemnation that has been built in your mind. You hold the key to freedom. Drop the judgments and lies against yourself. Let them go and allow the truth of God to set you free.

CHAPTER 19

DISAPPOINTMENT

It had been building over the past four years each time my cousin made yet another bad choice with yet another harsh consequence following. Each time the sad news came the disappointment would come and I would have to fight to regain my peace and resume standing in faith praying for his deliverance.

After many months of the cycle disappointment came to a head when a warrant was issued and he was arrested. This time it went beyond disappointment. I could taste the despair and I could not spit it out of my mouth. I knew that 1 Timothy 1:9 says that the law is not made for the righteous but for the lawless and disobedient. But I also knew that Timothy 1:15 says Christ Jesus came into the world to save the sinner. What I was struggling with was my emotions. I was tempted to go "flat line". Do you know what it is to go "flat line" emotionally? It is a form of denial and I had learned it at a young age.

Growing up some terrible things happened to me at the hand of people outside my immediate family. I learned to cope by not thinking about it. That was the only way I could control the pain, confusion and anger. If I did not think about it then I did not feel the emotions. It was what a little girl could do to cope and it helped me survive. The problem with that coping mechanism is that when you go "flat line" you feel nothing negative or positive. Life is just dull and empty. Many years ago, when I came to know Jesus and He started me on the inner healing and deliverance track. He slowly took me to those hard places and as I trusted Him and forgave, I was slowly able to feel again. He showed me that I could risk loving and being loved because He loved me and would help me, strengthen me and lift me up out of that dark and dull world. He had told me that going "flat line" was no longer an option. Therefore, I went to Him and He helped me to process the disappointment over my cousin.

The dictionary defines disappointment as an expectation not met; being let down, defeated, and downhearted. We all experience disappointments large and small with other people and with ourselves. And the disappointment can be about very legitimate expectations. It is part of the fallen nature. If it is a small disappointment, we can usually set it aside and move on. However, if the frequency and intensity of the disappointment increases or if it builds up over time disappointment can open the door to more than just a frustrated expectation. It can open the door to grief, disillusionment, discouragement, and despair. Think of Ruth and Naomi and their great disappointment at the loss of their husbands. David who had been anointed to be king spent fourteen years running from Saul who was jealous and driven to destroy him. Joseph anointed of God and favored of his father was betrayed by his brothers and sold into slavery. Peter was given the revelation that Jesus was the Christ, yet out of fear denied that he even knew Jesus and consequently fell into despair over what he had done.

Disappointment is a devouring spirit assigned to swallow hope and courage. It brings doubt about God's integrity and His promises. It causes us to doubt our ability to hear from God and robs us of peace and joy. Disappointment is part of a group of spirits that are oppressive; among them are apathy, despair, discouragement, heaviness, defeatism, depression, chronic weariness, loneliness and hopelessness. These spirits are tyrants and press us down, keeping us from enjoying life.

As human beings we will fail and disappoint each other and ourselves. If not processed one disappointment will build on another and compound the pain. Jesus said He did not entrust Himself to any man because He knew what was in man. But we can entrust ourselves to Him because He will never fail us. Jesus came to set us free from oppression and every trap and devouring assignment.

In Psalm 42 and 43 David says repeatedly, "Why are you cast down O my soul (inner self), why are you disquieted within me? Hope in God, for I will yet praise Him for He is the help of my countenance and my God." Hebrews 11:1 tells us that faith is the substance of things hoped for, the evidence of things not seen. In John 10:10 it is recorded that Jesus exposes the evil one. He said, "Satan comes to kill, steal and destroy. But I came that you might have life and have it in abundance." So, if Satan can rob us of hope then he can destroy our faith. He sends us the door opener of disappointment but his ultimate goal is to steal our hope and kill our faith.

Because the manifestation of our prayer has not come, we choose to set hope aside (defer it) and consequently our hearts get sick. We must choose to hold on to hope which is an earnest expectation of the thing God has promised us. We must consciously set our will to hope and not change the channel by the words of our mouth. This will protect our hearts from sickness and heartache. So, I gave all the disappointment, past and present, to the Lord. I told Him that I hated the grief and sorrow that it brings and that it is against my will to be disappointed.

Yes, we can choose what we think and what we feel just as we can choose what we do. The Lord told us to take every thought captive to the obedience of Christ and to choose whom we will serve. We can choose to think in line with the Word of God and not let our emotions rule us. We have the privilege to choose the good and hate the evil. Ruth, Naomi, David, Joseph and Peter all chose the good. Each of us must choose. No one can do it for us. We can encourage each other, share our experience and instruct each other but ultimately each person must make the choice. The instruction in 1 Peter 5:7 is to cast all our cares upon the Lord, because He cares for us. Each of us must choose to do it. I can't cast the care for you and you can't do it for me. The end result of disappointment is hopelessness and hopelessness will lead to death.

It was raining as I awoke just before dawn. I had been crying in my sleep. As I laid in bed listening to the rain, I suddenly heard the birds. Despite the rain they were welcoming the dawn of a new day. It was a song in the night, a song of hope in the midst of the rain. My tears in the night did not cancel out the new day. There was still an ounce of hope and strength to push away the darkness of disappointment. I opened my spirit to receive grace for a new day. I said to the Lord "I have hope because You are a good God and Your mercies are new every morning. You are a good Father and You love me. Your promises will not fail me because You love me. Through the rain the birds welcomed the dawn. Through my tears I welcome Your mercy for me and for those I love." As the rain cleansed the atmosphere so my tears cleansed my soul.

After I gave the Lord all the disappointment, I forgave all those who had disappointed me including my cousin. The Lord asked me, "What do you want?" I said "I want abundant life for me and for my cousin." Then I began to speak out (decree and declare) what I wanted and what my cousin was appointed to, not what I was disappointed about. I said, "It is against my will to be disappointed. I choose to be encouraged. I choose to hold on to hope. I decree that my cousin will hold on to hope. He will receive the love of the Father and serve the Lord Jesus Christ. His life is filled with divine appointments. The Lord has set them for him. I believe he will choose to keep those appointments, walk through those doors and welcome those encounters. The Holy Spirit opens those doors for him, brings him to them and gives him the grace to walk through them. Only Holy Spirit can prepare and orchestrate divine encounters. His timing is perfect, His preparation is meticulous and his execution precise. I believe my cousin will stop allowing what happened to him or what he has done to dictate who he is. He will repent and go back to the core of who God made him to be and to do all God destined him to do. He is highly favored and deeply loved. I choose to rest in God's love for me and His great love for him."

When I finished my declarations, I had stood against the devil and I was released from disappointment. I was at peace.

The Lord took me to Psalm 71:14 that says, "I choose to hope continually and will praise You yet more and more." I saw that scripture as the antidote for disappointment. So now I daily say: "I choose to hope continually and to praise the Lord more and more."

It must be a conscious act of our will to hope. Protecting our hearts from sickness, be it emotional, physical or spiritual is our responsibility. If hope is weak faith is weak. If hope is lost love is lost. Hope is the hinge that keeps us hooked to faith and love. Choose hope.

Thank God for who He is and what He has done. We are children of light and children of the day and let us, who are of the day be sober, putting on the breastplate of faith and love and for a helmet the hope of salvation (1 Thessalonians 5:7-8).

Deal with disappointments, both large and small immediately. Do not allow disappointment to get a foothold in your soul and rob you of hope and destroy your faith.

We make the choice and God is faithful to give us grace to overcome. It is God who helps us and strengthens us and lifts us up out of every disappointment. Hope is not lost. It is found in Jesus. "Hope deferred makes the heart sick; but when the desire comes, it is a tree of life" (Proverbs 13:12).

PART C

ALLEGORY OF
THE SHEEP

CHAPTER 20

WILLING HOSTAGE

Day melted into day as she struggled to survive the emptiness of her existence. She had trained herself to live in the moment. By not thinking about the past, its ability to torment her was minimized. Her heart ached for gentleness and refreshment. Her ears strained to hear a familiar voice only to be met by empty silence or the clamor of his ranting. Tender souls were never meant to live among cold, hard, jagged rocks. How had she come to this lifeless place? She decided to break the numbness and searched her mind in an effort to reconstruct the faded memories behind the veil of time and the bewitchment that overshadowed her so long ago.

There once had been joy at the dawn of each new day as the birds sang their greeting. Sunlight danced upon the dew-drenched leaves as she moved gracefully chasing butterflies from flower to flower. As free and happy as she had been, a deep longing for excitement had many times brought her to the edge of the meadow. Despite repeated warnings, she would venture out a little farther each day just to see what she would find.

On that fateful day she was on one of her little adventures when suddenly she heard an unfamiliar sound. A strong hissing followed by a threatening silence. She scanned the ground and as she turned a snake met her gaze as it slithered its way toward her. There were bushes on both sides and a boulder at her back. She was clearly cornered and the snake increased its thrust savoring her inability to escape. Suddenly from the boulder something lunged into the air and landed with one hoof squarely on the head of the snake. The little sheep stood frozen, both relieved and exhausted from the tension of the moment. In awe she watched the ram trample her enemy into the dust.

The ram was stronger and faster than any she had ever seen. He was rugged yet spoke softly to her. Each day he came to meet her at the edge of the meadow and her heart leaped with excitement when she heard his voice. She was flattered that he wanted to be with her and his daring thrilled her. He crossed the land so swiftly that it seemed like his hoofs never touched the ground. She followed wherever he went and was so awe struck that she failed to notice that all he talked about was himself, his exploits, his strength, his plans and dreams. The transition had been gradual and she had slipped into it without a struggle.

Each day the Shepherd warned her not to go and each day she met the ram at the edge of the meadow. Her friends pleaded with her to allow time to prove his character. But his charisma had wrapped itself around her and she could hear no voice but his. It never occurred to her to stop, she just floated along yielding to the attachment. His dreams filled the void for adventure in her soul. Deaf to the warnings of the Shepherd for caution she soon vowed to follow wherever the ram went. Although she acknowledged his narcissism, she chose to become a willing hostage convincing herself that he would one day come to care more about her than about himself.

The climb up the mountain had been gradual but grew harder with each new moon. Her only comfort was his warm body next to hers each night. Over time even that became sporadic as he spent days away leaving her isolated in a cold dark cave. Two other rams joined him in his quest for the ideal mountaintop. They too were seduced by his many words and grandiose dreams but over time they became disillusioned and slipped away. What he searched for was always just beyond the next ridge. He became increasingly frustrated as each ridge grew more difficult to scale and failed to produce nirvana. She had tried so hard to please him believing that if she did everything, he wanted he would be content and they could live the life she once imagined. That lie was as big as his lies about where he had been and when he would return. His need for attention was as unquenchable as the unstableness of his mind. Intoxicated by his delusions of grandeur he exploded at the slightest perceived rejection.

Her already parched soul was grieved each time his frustration erupted into rage. His efforts to control life only served to fuel the fires of his disappointment and rage irrupted with little warning. Stunned by the force she could not move or speak the day his horns turned on her. The heated moment having passed he vowed never to hurt her again. He nursed her wounds and condemned himself. Despite his resolve and promises he would revert to violence with little provocation and the little sheep learned to keep her distance. The gulf between them grew as great as the unbearable isolation. Her mind was now so severely oppressed that she began to entertain the idea that the real problem was not his abuse but rather her inability to cope with it. What had been a dream of adventure had become a nightmare of distortion.

Suddenly she came out of her rambling memories. As she looked up, she saw a small patch of flowers growing between two rocks. Their beauty flooded her with yearning for the meadow and the sheepfold. Tears gushed uncontrollably and almost drowned her in sorrow as she remembered how the Shepherd had slept at the door of the sheepfold each night to guard the sheep. With little confidence that he would hear her she cried out for Him to rescue her from this ruthless and terrible tyrant.

That evening the ram did not return to the cave. Alone and broken she fell into a deep sleep. In her dream she saw herself standing alone in front of the cave on the rocky mountain. A ray of sunlight highlighted the path they had taken many years before. As she followed the light, she saw each step of disappointment that had brought her to this cave. A lizard moved quickly across her path, and a pebble went bouncing down the sunlit path to the base of the mountain. She could hear the voice of the Shepherd calling to her, "I love you little sheep. Come home." She woke up with a start, and a surge of hope filled her heart.

As the sunrise peaked over the ridge, she walked to the edge of the cave. Looking down the mountain the truth came to her like drops of rain. No amount of patience or compassion had changed his rage. He devoured everything in his path and she would not be an exception. If the Shepherd had been standing there, the ram would have found the control not to rage and not to attack her. He had not changed because he did not want to change. The descent off the mountain would be no harder than the climb up and the risk no greater than that of living with his abuse. He who had once spoken so tenderly to her had become a threat and his horns would ultimately destroy her. Her struggle to cope with his anger was not the problem. His abuse was the problem. Selfishness and control were at his core and she had to make a change. Not because he was selfish but because he could not be trusted. She had given him her life and he had repeatedly violated her trust.

She realized that the Shepherd had always loved her. He had never hurt her or tried to control her. He had not forsaken her. She had chosen to walk away from Him and the safety of the sheepfold. In the depths of her desperation her soul cried out with words that could not be uttered. She had given herself as prey to the horns of the ram, now she cried out to escape as a bird from the trap of the hunter. If the ram could hear the voice of the Shepherd there would be hope, but his rage blocked his ears and hardened his heart. Despite her pain, fear and disappointment she could still hear all the words the Shepherd had spoken to her, the playful words, the endearing words and the warnings too. They ran through her mind and she held on to them now as treasures in the darkness. He had been crying out to her but only now could she hear Him clearly. He called to her lovingly, "Don't be afraid; you belong to Me. You always have. Return to Me. I will heal you and strengthen you. I love you, but you must decide and you must take the first step."

For several weeks she rested and strengthened her body and her resolve. She waited for a time when the ram would cycle into his three or four days of isolation. When that time came, she began her descent determined not to look back and not to fear the future.

Two days into her trek the ram appeared. He was not angry, as she had expected but tender and pleading. She refused to be moved by his words. She had listened to them for too long only to be repeatedly betrayed. She had no defense against his physical strength but she preferred to die trying to escape than continue to die slowly day-by-day. To her surprise he turned away and began thrashing his horns against the rocks. She knew him well and refused to be deterred by his self-abasement. She continued her descent until the noise of his thrashing and his words were a faint echo. The voice of the Shepherd saying "I love you. Come home. "kept her resolve strong.

On the third day of her descent she fainted from exhaustion. Her hoofs were bloody and her body thin. She fell to the ground weak and vulnerable. Other sheep had seen her in the distance and rallied together waiting for her rescue. When she awoke the Shepherd was carrying her down the mountain and back to the meadow. The safety of His arms flooded her with peace. His heartbeat calmed her fears and her tears washed away the grief. He did not scold her or speak harshly to her. In the clear water of the stream He gently washed away her shame and cleaned her wounds. She drifted in and out of sleep as He sang over her. His love left no room for condemnation and she was finally able to rest from the constant vigilance.

The birds sang and the dew glistens on the sunlit leaves again. She had come home not richer but humbled and broken. It seemed like another lifetime ago. A dream that started out by her enjoying his brute strength and adventure while ignoring the foolishness had ended as a bad dream from which she had now awakened. Never again would she listen to the lies of manipulation. Time healed her body and the love of the Sheppard healed her soul. He taught her to forgive the ram and then herself. He never reproached her for leaving. She had exercised compassion without limits for the ram but had failed to set boundaries for herself. She had become a coward hiding behind a veil of grief. But ultimately, she had come out from behind the veil and chose to become responsible for her own well-being. At the risk of his rage she had enforced the sanctity of her own personhood.

She had been queen for a day. First there was an eclipse of the sun and her soul was obscured by his charisma. Then there was an eclipse of the moon and she was caught in the shadow of his dark soul. Her joy withdrew and her own light was overshadowed by his control and selfishness. She had been a queen to whom no one paid homage. It was a process but in time songs in the night returned and gladness of heart bore sprouts.

The Shepherd had not left her; she had abandoned Him. He had never stopped looking for her and calling out to her; she had turned a deaf ear to His warnings. His voice had finally reached her when she humbled herself and cried out for help. She had abandoned the love and protection of the Shepherd and the sheepfold for the idol she had made of the ram. The idol was crushed and the fantasy turned nightmare ended. With renewed strength came better choices and the deep satisfaction of having had the courage to change. With the help of the Shepherd she began to build a better and richer life one choice at a time. The first choice was to forgive the ram and the second was to forgive herself. Only by the love extended to her and the strength of the

Shepherd could she do either. The way she got in was the way she got out, by choice.

"Though I walked in the midst of trouble, the Lord has preserved my life. He has stretched out his hand to help me, to save me" (Psalm 138:7).

CHAPTER 21

THE POWER OF CHOICE

The greatest gift we have each received is the gift of choice. Choice is a spiritual law and is what sets us apart from the rest of creation. We have the opportunity to choose life or death. When a situation presents its self, we have the option to exercise our free will and that option is processed through our soul (mind, will and emotions). Day by day and moment by moment we choose to obey or disobey the Word of God.

IF WE CHOOSE LIFE, WE CHOOSE HOLY SPIRIT GUIDANCE

The Holy Spirit desires our participation. His grace gives us the ability to be wise and choose the good thing. The wages we receive for good choices are that those choices produce life, truth, love, joy peace, freedom and well-being. We will be blessed.

IF WE CHOOSE DEATH, WE CHOOSE DEMONIC SPIRIT GUIDANCE

Demonic spirits will use deception and demand control. They bring fear, torment, self-righteousness, rebellion, wickedness, assault and dishonor. The wages we will earn from this choice will be death, which includes deception, compromise, hatred, grief, torment and oppression. We will be cursed.

God said that He calls heaven and earth to witness against us, that He has set before us life and death, the blessing and the curse. He advises us to choose life in order that we may live, but it is still our choice (Duet 30:19).

"Seek first the kingdom of God and His righteousness and all these things will be added to you" (Matt 6:33-34). To you has been given the mystery of the kingdom of God... the mystery of God's way of being and doing things. There is a specific path to get to the desired end. God has plans for us and Satan has plans for us. We get to choose which plan we will align with. Jesus is the way to abundant life. All other ways end in death, loss and destruction (John 14:6 & John 10:10).

OBEDIENCE:

The Prophet Samuel said "Does the Lord delight in burnt offerings and sacrifices as much as in obeying the voice of the Lord? To obey is better than sacrifice, and to heed is better than sacrifice" (1 Sam 15:22). James admonishes us to not merely listen to the Word, and so deceive ourselves, but to be doers of the Word (James 1:22).

From time to time we may find ourselves in a dry place. We do not seem to be hearing the voice of the Lord or are not connected to Him as we once were. If that happens back up to the last thing God told you to do. If you will choose to repent and then do what He told you His grace and blessings will begin to flow again.

DISOBEDIENCE IS REBELLION:

Rebellion is defined as an uprising intended to overthrow an existing government or ruling authority; an act of defiance toward authority (Webster's Dictionary). Rebellion is the spirit of antichrist – it is not only disobedience but it is also disrespect for authority. Lucifer, originally one of the archangels, was expelled from heaven because he wanted to attract to himself the glory and worship that was rightfully due to God alone. He then became known as Satan, the adversary. One third of the angelic hosts joined in the rebellion with Satan and were also expelled from heaven. On earth Satan continued his rebellion against God by tempting man to disobey God. Adam joined in the rebellion and became alienated from his Creator. Man, then became vulnerable to Satan and his demons. These powers of darkness have no flesh life of their own and seek to occupy the bodies of men and women in order to pursue their rebellion against God.

Rebellion is rooted in pride and if not dealt with will result in lawlessness. Thinking that we have a right to sit in judgment of those in authority over us is the same sin that Lucifer committed against God. This includes criticism of ministers, government, parents, employers etc.

1 Samuel 15:23 states that rebellion is as the sin of witchcraft. Witchcraft is the use of sorcery or magic, communication with demons or with familiar spirits, a fascination with enchantment. Divination is seeking power or knowledge from any spirit

source other than the Holy Spirit. God hates divination because it leads people to seek satanic intelligence for guidance in their lives instead of trusting God.

Critical attitudes and rejection are a subtle form of manipulation and control. Underlying manipulation is a threat that is aimed at control. It is rebellion against God's plan and purpose for mankind and destroys the free will that God has given to each one of us. Violation of the free will of an individual to be the person God has planned and purposed them to be is rebellion against God. Manipulation, domination and control are the tools of witchcraft. It is not surprising, therefore, that the victim of manipulation, domination and control can be demonized as a result. Violence against another person, anorexia, drug abuse, overworking is all rebellion against the law of love against ourselves or against others.

Rebellion can come in through music lyrics that deliver a message of rebellion against established order, especially against civil law. Sometimes rebellion, in the form of refusal to conform or cooperate or in irrational anger, can be a consequence of sexual abuse. Healing the wounds of abuse will be necessary in order to be delivered from the rebellion.

We are to rightly divide the Word of God taught to us. We are to judge with righteous judgment. We are not to sit in the seat of the scoffer but we are to test the spirits. We can only do all this if we know the Word and have the Holy Spirit to give us revelation of its meaning and application.

Rebellion is a gatekeeper. It opens the way for other evil spirits to enter our souls or bodies. Demonic spirits that are tied to rebellion are: self-will. stubbornness, disobedience and anti-submissiveness.

STUBBORNNESS:

Unreasonably determined to exact one's will; persistent; difficult to handle (Webster Dictionary).

The Lord called the children of Israel a stiff-necked people. They were told to go in and possess the promised land. Because of fear and unbelief, they refused to obey and wandered in the desert for 40 years. Only Joshua and Caleb believed God and lived through that generation. God said that they were of a different spirit.

Korah was a descendent of Levi and leader of the rebellion against his cousins Moses and Aaron. He and all his followers perished in an earthquake and flames of fire. Why did they rebel? Because of jealousy and offense. Korah and his company were excluded from the office of priesthood and were assigned to the "inferior" service of the tabernacle (Numbers 16 and 26: 9-11).

Pharaoh was stubborn even at the expense of his own comfort and that of his people. When the plague of the frogs hit Egypt, Moses asked him "When should I entreat for you and destroy the frogs?" Pharaoh answered, "tomorrow." He slept with the frogs one more night because of his pride. Pharaoh hardened his heart until there was no more remedy (Exodus 7 to Exodus 10).

The people of Sodom and Gomorrah hardened their hearts to righteousness and were destroyed because of their sexual perversion (Gen 19:8). The sons of Eli hardened their hearts to the Levitical law and both they and their father died (1 Sam 2:22-25).

"He that being often reproved, hardens his neck shall suddenly be destroyed, and that without remedy" (Proverbs 29:1).

MERCY:

"I have called you back from the ends of the earth so you can serve me. For I have chosen you and will not throw you away" (Isaiah 41:9). It is God's will that none should perish but that all come to repentance. Rebellion is an issue of self-will, which has become embedded in the heart. A hardened heart is a terrible thing. Pray for a heart change, for a softening of the heart, for a breaking of self-will. The love of God has made a way of escape even for the most hardened heart. Ask for all ground given over to unclean spirits through rebellion be cancelled and cleansed by the blood of Jesus.

REPENTANCE:

"Be clothed with humility for God resists the proud, and gives grace to the humble" (1 Peter 5:5). Repentance is humbling, admitting that we are wrong, asking for forgiveness and forgiving others is humbling. The primary reason for confession is for our benefit. When we confess our sins, we come into agreement with God that what we did or failed to do was in rebellion against his law of love. God wants us restored to mercy and grace by our choice to let go of rebellion and stubbornness and submit to humility and obedience.

Satan can't cross our will. If we choose not to be afraid or not to lie or not to be offended no one can force us to do it. Our power is in choosing to exercise our personal will over and against the will of rebellion. As we read the Word and see what the will of the Lord is, we can decree and declare what we choose. For example, we can read 1 Peter 5:5 and say "I choose to be clothed with humility. It is against my will to be proud. I choose to receive the grace of God by being humble. It is against my will to be stubborn. I choose to admit when I am wrong."

Inner Healing is a choice to commit to the long-term process of rebuilding the dignity that has been shattered in our lives. Do not question your right to object to mistreatment, especially if you have mistreated yourself. Emotional and verbal abuse and manipulation by others are masked violence. Choose to protest and insist on your God given right to respect and to the right to become all that God created you to be.

The mandate to all who have been healed and delivered is found in 2nd Timothy 2:25-26: "In humility instructing those that oppose themselves in the hope that God may grant them repentance to the acknowledgement of the truth, that they may recover themselves out of the trap of the devil that has taken them captive at his will."

CHAPTER 22

I WANT A KING

(Evelyn's story)

Jehoshaphat started out well as King of Judah. He did what was right in God's eyes and the Lord blessed him. However, toward the end of his life he aligned himself with the ungodly King Ahaziah in order to build ships. The ships were wrecked and so was the end of his life (2 Chronicles).

Solomon started out well. There was prosperity and wisdom in his reign. But after he had built the temple of the Lord and amassed great wealth his heart turned from the Lord. The Lord had said that the children of Israel were not to intermarry with foreign women. Solomon disobeyed and his many foreign wives turned his heart away from the Lord. He did evil in the sight of the Lord by building high places and offering incense and sacrifices to their idols (1Kings 11). It took 400 years for the nation of Israel to rid itself of the idols.

Jehu was a mighty warrior. He destroyed Jezebel and tore down the Baal altars and killed all the priest of Baal (2 Kings 9). Although a mighty man the scriptures tell us that he continued in the sin of Jeroboam. What was that sin? The people were to go to Jerusalem to worship at the temple of the Lord. Jeroboam was afraid of losing the people under him so he built two golden calves, one at Bethel and one at Dan and appointed priest to offer sacrifice there. He cast the Word of God behind his back and caused the kingdom of Israel to sin eventually splitting the nation.

Each king ended up terribly wrong because he was in rebellion against the Word of the Lord. Some because of lust, some because of greed and others because of deception; but each because they cast the Word of the Lord behind their backs. Acts 20:29 warns us to be on guard for savage wolves who will distort the truth in order to draw people to themselves to justify or excuse sin.

Evelyn had lived six years as a new believer, being taught the Word of God and learning the ways of the Lord. Then she met such a wolf at a singles group. They attended a conference together and before she knew it, she was convinced she could not live without him. He was handsome, talented and very charismatic. Friends and ministers tried to caution her to slow down but she would not listen.

The two agreed to tell each other everything about their past and spent long hours sharing their life experiences. She had great compassion for his poor and abusive childhood. He had told her of his struggle with drugs as a teenager and that one night he had thrown them into the river and never looked back. It was a short four-month whirlwind courtship before she married him. Evelyn believed his words because she wanted to believe them. She desperately wanted to be married and did not wait long enough to see if his words matched his actions. A few months later she decided to surprise him by cleaning his garage. Sadly, she was the one surprised when she found his stash of drugs. Her heart was sick with disappointment...with him, but especially with herself. Obviously at some point he had looked back and retrieved the drugs and no doubt he had lied to her about much more.

The king's smile is his favor but if the king is not noble, if he is deceptive his smile is a trap. Feeling betrayed and ensnared Evelyn fell into a pit of depression that lasted many years. But what predisposed her to be attracted to this man and to stay with him for many years? It was the kinks in her armor. She could not be objective because she wanted a king and she gave her heart away quickly because she was lonely. Evelyn wanted change, adventure and excitement. She got them all but it was a horrible rollercoaster ride. She was in love with the idea of marriage and caught up with him internally, which was idolatry and addiction of another sort. He could quote full chapter of the Bible, but she failed to notice the verses he skipped. Professing his loyalty to Jesus and singing worship music all the while deceiving her and using drugs. The signs had all been there but she was to blind to see them because of her desire for a husband. When she confronted him, he twisted the scriptures to justify his actions and refused to admit he had an addiction problem. He continually cast the Word of God behind his back.

His tongue, which had been so soft and flattering, became a sharp razor. His deception and manipulation were a greater offense then the addiction. He was deceitful about why he went from job to job and where he spent his time and why the bank account never balanced. At the root of all the lies was his rebellion against the Word of God. He was skilled at manipulation and often by not saying anything he let her make assumptions and took advantage of her compassion. At other times he would tell her what she wanted to hear and used flattery to get her to do what he wanted. He cloaked his deception with a veneer of religion. She tried to reason with him, prayed and fasted for him, argued with him, and offered to get help but his heart was hardened. He refused to allow the breath of truth to penetrate his soul.

Some of his skewed teachings were that there was no need for him to sit under a pastor or teacher because the Holy Spirit in him was his pastor and teacher. There was no need to tithe because God owned everything and did not need his money. He had liberty to do whatever he wanted as long as he did not come under the dominion of it. The problem with that was that he never could go more than three days without drugs or a day without alcohol. In other words, no accountability, no responsibility and license to do whatever he wanted. Mary Jane, Crack and Jose Cuervo had turned his heart away from God and he influenced other young men to join him.

Evelyn did not know it then, but eventually realized that the Jezebel and Delilah spirits operate through a man just as through a woman. Seduction, manipulation, control, isolation, and flattery all operate in either gender. He tried to live a double life and was greedy for material and financial gain. Ultimately, he used her to support him and stole her joy and hope. She stayed with him because she had compassion without limits. She convinced herself that if she loved him enough and prayed enough, he would change. In an effort to protect herself she spent long hours at work and isolated herself. Fear of making another mistake paralyzed her and caused her much anguish of soul. She was stressed, strained and tremendously lonely. Evelyn asked the Lord, "Can you change the heart of a man?" And the Lord answered, "Yes, I can do all things." She then asked, "Will you change the heart of this man?" God replied, "It depends on the man, because he has free will." Unfortunately, her king turned dictator never chose to change.

Natural pearls are formed in the oyster from irritation and adversity. Her relationship with this man had plenty of both. She was married to that deceiver for a dozen years and the test and trials were tremendous as she experienced the vexation of soul the scriptures speak of. She never joined him in his drug and alcohol use and as the years passed, they became like two ships passing in the night. She did not leave him because of the addiction or because of the lack of emotional, financial or spiritual support, not even because of the other women. Evelyn left him because he could not be trusted. It was her valley of the shadow of death experience and the Lord was faithful to walk her through the chaos and rescue her from a ruthless and terrible tyrant.

Proverbs 6:16-19 teaches us that pride has seven heads. It has haughty eyes, a lying tongue, sheds innocent blood and its heart devises wickedness. Its feet run to mischief, it is a false witness and will sow discord among brothers. The 40th chapter of the book of Job exposes the children of pride as those who operate in superiority, self-promotion, haughtiness, boasting, arrogance, and are self-serving. They are jealous, angry, condescending, independent, boastful, dishonor authority and desire to be served. They seek a reputation and use any position of authority to control others. Pride is lodged in the will and ultimately destroys its victims.

The only remedy to pride and all of its children is to choose a life of humility (James 4:10). Only by being totally dependent on the Holy Spirit and by being patient for His direction, can we be spared the deep pits of life. If we miss it, we have to be humble enough to admit it and ask the Lord for wisdom and a strategy in order to escape the trap.

His outbursts became so violent and the finances so strained that Evelyn was finally forced to leave. Only when she got away from him was, she able to think clearly and see what he did, what she allowed and what she had to do to recover her life. When his voice stopped and she was alone Evelyn was able to hear the Lord. Over the next few years the Holy Spirit helped her to be honest about submission having been one-sided and that she had failed to create a crisis in his life. Evelyn came to realize that she had yielded to emotions instead of justice because she was engrossed in him. She was a coward hiding behind a curtain of denial, shame, obligation and religion. She had lost sight of the fact that she was as important as he was in the relationship and she had failed to protect herself by not objecting to his mistreatment. She had not enforced her right to be safe and had not set healthy boundaries. It was all a great blow to her to admit she had wasted so many years but the humbling and the honesty was her way out of captivity. She forgave him more easily then she forgave herself, but in time that too came.

As a child of God Evelyn was a person of value and her Heavenly Father wanted to bless her. But her part was to stay in her Father's house. Her going into the street looking for a king and hooking up with a wolf did not change her father's love for her. Just as with her husband the Lord did not violate her free will. She had to make the choice to bring her mistakes to him as well as her many questions. The Father forgave her and healed her wounds. Over time the answers came or were no longer important. Her soul was restored and she was gently and carefully guided back to the Father's house and to her rightful place of dignity. It was the Lord's mercy that she was not consumed because His compassions fail not, they are new every morning. Great is His faithfulness (Lamentations 3:22-23). Evelyn came to understand that the only honest, kind and faithful king was Jesus and she would never give his place to a man again.

Ask the Lord to forgive you if you have operated in pride and deception. Repent and renounce it as sin if you have deceived or manipulated others. Ask Him to deliver you and give you grace to humble yourself. If you are the one who has been deceived ask the Lord to remove the deception and manipulation. In the Name of Jesus break the power of any agreement that is an unholy alliance and ask the Holy Spirit to give you wisdom and discernment. Cry out for it as you would for water in a desert so that you will not spend years in a wilderness as Evelyn did.

CHAPTER 23

SELF-PITY

(Myra's story)

It seems ironic that the women I met last night described me as being "together" yet the person I saw in the mirror as I got ready for bed was far from that perception. She was evaluating my outward appearance not the one who lives inside my skin. Before I went to sleep, I asked the Lord to show me why what she saw and what I saw were worlds apart.

The Lord answered my request with a dream. In the dream I saw a young girl wandering from room to room in a very large empty house. There were no drapes, no furniture and no people. Exhausted from the search she decided to stop and wait by the door in hope that someone would eventually come in. The strange thing was that when she walked over to stand behind the door she shrank. She was no taller than the three-inch base-board. Then she heard a voice say: "You had better not stand behind the door. Someone may hit you with it when they come in." When I woke up, I knew that I was that girl and throughout the day the Holy Spirit gave me the interpretation of the dream.

My parents were too busy, or perhaps empty themselves, to give me much emotional nourishment. I don't know that I ever heard them say I was unwanted, but I seemed to always know that to be the case. Their careers were paramount. I never lacked for things but I always lacked connection. Alone on the inside I went from place to place looking for someone to connect with but I always came up empty. The Lord was warning me not to stay hidden behind the door any longer.

The next day as I drove to work, I saw a billboard on the highway and one word stood out to me like a neon sign... "IN-SIGNIFICANT." I had asked the Lord to show me why I saw myself as being three inches tall and what He revealed was loneliness, emptiness and insignificance. I was stuck and no one could help me if I did not risk coming out from behind the door and becoming known. I felt like I was three inches tall on the inside and no one could see me. Or is it that I could not see myself? Even if I dared to ask for what I needed no one could hear such a small voice. I just slipped in and out unobserved and untouched. So, I prayed again and asked the Holy Spirit to give me courage to come out from behind the door and seek to be healed.

When I went in for healing prayer I knew exactly where to begin. I had to start at the point when I had gone behind the door. I had to start with Arthur. We met at the high school pool. I was sixteen and he was seventeen. I remember twisting my ring around and around my finger as he spoke to me. I could not believe that someone as handsome and talented could spend his time talking with me. He was a superstar on the basketball court and he frightened and excited me all at the same time. I was so captivated that I followed his every step. When he asked me to the winter formal I froze in disbelief.

The limo was crowded, and the music loud, so I just had to sit and look pretty. When we arrived, I was relieved that everyone kept coming up and talking with him because I didn't have to work up something to say. I had a few whirlwind months of fun with Arthur and his friends and for the first time in my life I started to connect. One afternoon I called his home, and his mother answered the phone. It was obvious she had been crying. When I asked what was wrong, she broke into sobs and hung up. I ran to his house only to find an ambulance, police cars and the yard roped off with yellow tape. I stood in numb disbelief as a body was carried out covered with a sheet and placed in the ambulance. Arthur had been found locked in his room dead of a self-inflicted wound. Shockwaves hit the school at the news but his parents never disclosed the reason behind his suicide. The superstar whom we all admired was riddled with hopelessness and despair and no one could tell me why.

I buried myself in my bed and cried until my head hurt more than my heart. I had no way to explain what had happened to him or to me. All I knew was that I could never risk connecting to anyone like that again. I had given my heart away and I could not get it back. I have since forgiven him and I had tried to forget but that hollow sadness has lived inside me and has grown with each passing year. As warped as it sounds that grief is the only connection I have with him. I had bouts of emotional outbursts at first but they soon gave way to pining and eventual deadness in my emotions. That tragedy threw me into a large pit of depression and I have been stuck there ever since. I guess I stay numb so that I won't recycle through the anger and despair again. Grief and self-pity are so interlocked that I can't tell one from the other.

When I read Psalm 31 it was like a pane of glass reflecting my condition. It reads: "Because of grief my soul and body are weakened. I am forgotten like a dead man; and out of mind like a broken vessel. My life is spent with sorrow and my years with sighing." But like King David I cried out to the Lord and He heard my voice and answered me.

Since Myra started her healing journey the Lord has used the scriptures to not only expose her condition but to show her the way out of it. She learned the difference between grief that leads to accepting what happened and self-pity that kept her stuck in isolation. She had believed a three-fold lie, and like a three-fold cord, it was not easily broken. By the grace of God, it came undone one cord at a time. First the lie that she was beyond help broke, secondly the lie that her situation was hopeless dissolved and finally the lie that no one, not even God, could help her was exposed and destroyed.

Like a little child, she had run into her room and refused to be comforted by hiding behind the door. She was deceived to think that self-pity was grieving. As she studied the scriptures, she began to see that grieving ends. It ended for David when his son died and it ended for the people of Israel when Moses died. Her grief had never ended and she had to ask herself why. Slowly the realization came that she had chosen to put herself in the prison of isolation for fear of risking the pain of loss again.

She was shocked when the Holy Spirit convicted her of self-pity being prideful. She chose to forgive Arthur for leaving her and had to acknowledge that she was so angry that she refused to allow God to comfort her. She refused to allow the truth that Jesus carried her grief to be reality in her life in order to keep the ungodly connection with a dead man. Suddenly she saw that as arrogance personified. Myra came to accept what happened and released it. She is no longer a teenager, three inches tall standing behind the door. She has repented of pride, renounced self-pity and all that goes with it. Myra has been set free to risk meeting whoever walks through the door of her life.

We all go through the valley of the shadow of death many times in life; sometimes deeply and sometimes momentarily. Whatever the depth of our loss, we must turn to the Lord quickly. He alone can take us safely through the valley as we adjust to a new reality. He alone can give us the strength and courage to move on. Jesus came to heal the brokenhearted but we must choose to allow Him to heal us. He gave us his Word and sent the Holy Spirit to comfort us. We are admonished in scripture to not be overcome by a spirit of grief. Wearing that cloak for too long a time will open the door to a trap set to enslave us and self-pity will cause us to become disabled emotionally.

"He (Jesus) was despised and rejected by men, a man of sorrows and acquainted with grief. And we hid, as it were, our faces from Him; He was despised, and we did not esteem Him. Surely, He has borne our grief and carried our sorrows; yet we esteemed Him stricken, smitten by God, and afflicted" (Isaiah 53:3-4).

"Come to me all you that are weary and heavy laden and I will give you rest for your souls" (Matt 11:28).

Prayer you can pray if this applies to your life:

"Father God, I come to you in the name of Jesus and I renounce self-pity and pride. I ask You to forgive me for not allowing You to comfort and heal me. I ask You to forgive me for holding on to grief. I accept Your forgiveness and yield my soul to You for restoration. Give me courage to accept what I cannot change, release the past and to keep on looking forward living in hope. As I read Your Word renew my mind to truth and give me grace to walk in it. Amen."

CHAPTER 24

RAIN DROPS OF KINDNESS

(Helen's story)

Our corporate office was in dire need of a facelift. It had been years since anyone had addressed the need for paint and carpet and I was assigned to be the project manager for the task. My organizational skills kicked into high gear as I plotted out a course. I enjoyed the challenge as an escape from the monotony of routine computer work. The Lord was faithful to send me good movers, suppliers and contractors and the project was moving along smoothly. Two weeks into the assignment the Lord showed up with a surprise. It was so unexpected that I am sure it would have thrown me into a tailspin had it not been for my having been paying attention to the Holy Spirit.

I was taping up phone cords and marking file cabinets as an attractive man stood painting the molding around a window across the room. We talked about the weather and the new flooring as we worked. He spoke in a gentle unhurried voice as the conversation took a more personal turn. He was originally from Canada and planned to return there when his children reached the age of 21. It was obvious that he was heartbroken over the loss of his marriage and that he missed his family. I felt compassion for him and in my heart asked the Lord to comfort him in his loss and to heal his broken heart. Suddenly I felt the warmth of the Holy Spirit flood over my own soul. It was a parallel like that of a railroad track. What I was praying for him had suddenly come upon me. Our conversation was interrupted by a phone call and we each went about our business.

As I left for lunch a short time later, I realized that I had definitely been impacted emotionally and I needed to get in touch with what had just happened. This was not about the painter but about me. It was not the words this man had spoken but the way they were delivered that had touched my soul. His manner was strong but his words were gentle and kind. I could see that what I had prayed for him was what I needed for myself and I became acutely aware of how bankrupt my soul was for comfort and healing. In that moment I felt extremely vulnerable.

My father loved me but was a critical and domineering person who ran our home with an iron fist of intimidation. He suffered bouts of deep depression and was emotionally volatile. My first husband seemed incapable of dialogue. In ten years of marriage I do not remember ever connecting with him heart to heart. Although an academic genius he was a closet alcoholic who escaped into a bottle. His emotions were shut away behind a door to which I was not given access. My second husband had a very charismatic personality but was double minded; hot and cold, calculating and deceptive. I had married one person only to find I lived with two. His words were used as instruments to gain personal advantage and were spoken with a hard edge of defiance or a smooth coating of manipulation. The men in my life had been emotionally broken by the wounding of their childhood. They had been scarred by life and became hardened and incapable of tenderness. Was it any wonder that I was like a desert wasteland desperate for the soft rain of kindness?

How many other women walk around parched and empty? Responding to romance novels or romance movies because of the longing in their souls for a gentle word from a man. Even the affection of children is not capable of meeting the need a woman has for the tenderness of a man. We surround ourselves with soft light, silk sheets, fluffy towels and fragrant flowers in an effort to comfort ourselves. Romance is what we call it but kindness and tenderness is what we really seek. Trinkets and luxury are a menial substitute for the real comfort of a tender-hearted man. "What is desired of a man is his kindness" (Proverbs 19:22 a).

The desire of my heart is to be kind to others to speak words that will comfort and heal. I know that it is impossible for me to give what I do not have. That night I prayed and asked Jesus, the most tender, kind and loving Man alive to comfort me. I forgave the men in my life for not watering me with their words. I opened my heart and soul to be healed of the harsh words they had spoken to me and of the labels placed over me through their judgments. I released them from their obligation and asked the Lord to forgive them and heal their brokenness as well as mine. "Be ye kind one to another, tenderhearted, forgiving one another, even as God for Christ's sake has forgiven you." (Ephesians 4:32)

Are you an empty vessel into which no kind word has been deposited? Are you parched and broken because harsh or empty words have filled your cup? Jesus is the living water who can fill you and refresh you with His kindness and affection. In the film *David the Hunted* Abigail says to David, "I was a parched land until you turned and spoke to me." I too was as a parched land until Jesus turned and spoke to me. Let Him speak to you. His words are life and His love unending. Allow Him to heal your broken heart and fill you with His kindness. "His mouth is most sweet: yes, He is altogether lovely. This is my beloved and this is my friend" (Song of Solomon 5:16 a).

I have since met men who have tender hearts and the capacity to extend true kindness. Some are young, some old, some married and others single. They do exist on this planet but the Lord did not allow me to meet them until I forgave those who could not meet my needs and acknowledged my own depravation. Having allowed Jesus to fill me with His kindness and tenderness I now realize that those who do have that grace are reflecting what Christ has placed within them.

What are the depths to which emotional brokenness can take a person? Let me answer that question by telling you about Helen. As a child Helen had always felt self-conscious. She was awkward and her freckles and red hair did not allow her to blend in or hide. Her older brother who was handsome and popular was her chief mocker. At every opportunity he let her know what an embarrassment she was to him.

When she was fourteen her parents died in an auto accident and she was devastated. She went to live with her aunt who met all her physical needs and encouraged her to excel in academics but was stoic and void of affection. The only redeeming factor in the process was that her brother went to live with another family member.

Helen worked hard in high school and college allowing no time for social life or developing any long-term relationships. She hid in academia. After college she took a position with a well-established law firm. She eventually married one of the partners in the firm who was 20 years her senior. He reminded her of her father both in appearance and temperament. They had a child and motherhood took the place of intimacy with her husband. He was a good man but seemed incapable of understanding her deep need for affection and romance.

When her son left for military school it left a huge void in her soul. Her husband was preoccupied with running his growing law practice and never noticed how lonely and parched she was. To fill the void Helen volunteered in several hospital and church groups. One group was a jail ministry. Over time she started going to the prison to visit one of the inmates independent of the ministry group. She knew what she was doing was wrong but she refused to let go of the fantasy she had created in her mind. The inmate listened to her and said what she needed to hear. His words were food to her starving soul and she could not get enough of them.

After nine months she found herself in her car on a country road under a large oak tree with a gun in her lap. She cried until she thought her head would explode. How could she face another day now that her sand castle had been demolished? She had been a fool to think that someone could actually love her. The words he had said to her made her believe that was possible but what he had done prove otherwise. It was unclear to her now how much he had said and how much she had imagined. But she had been counting the days when he would be released. She had even visited his family and planned a celebration. When the time drew near, he purposely incited a fight and got caught with drugs. His parole was canceled and she was demoralized and swimming in despair as she drove out to the country intending to end her life. She struggled with herself and the demon of suicide for hours. Finally, she threw the gun in the back seat and drove home.

Confessing to her husband what she had almost done and why she had contemplated suicide she felt a release of the guilt she had been carrying. After collecting himself from the shock her husband went to her car, retrieved the gun, drove her to the hospital and put her in a 72-hour lockdown. Many hours of counseling exposed the depth of her emotional involvement with the inmate. In time her husband was able to forgive her and insisted she cut off all contact with the inmate and continue with counseling.

Many months passed and she never went back to the prison but she did not close the PO Box and continued to correspond with him. She made a conscious decision to continue the relationship and refused to let go of him in her heart. She justified her behavior to herself because the man had words she needed. Regardless of the fantasy she would not let go of the only one who had ever spoken words that filled the broken places in her soul.

Eventually she lost both men. Her husband died of a broken heart and the inmate wearied of the game and stopped writing. She then tried to see him but he refused her visits. She convinced herself that she had failed him and had caused him to reject her. She was sure that in time he would forgive her and reach out to her again. That day never came, but she still refused to release him from her heart.

Temptation comes from the inside. We are drawn away from what is noble by our own lusts and desires which are triggered by our brokenness. There has to be a hook, some void yearning to be satisfied that draws us away from what we know to be right. In Helen's case it was a huge cavern of emotional bankruptcy. She fell headlong into it with no restraint because her soul was void of affection from a man. She held on to what might have been and was operating in self-deception.

Agreement is made in the heart. Both Helen and the inmate had a need and used each other to meet the need with no regard to how they impacted each other or her husband. It was not love. It was fantasy lust and emotional perversion. Many times, in the course of this situation Helen had been offered the mercy of God through prayer, inner healing and deliverance. If she agreed to receive the mercy of God, she would have to give up her fantasy and she refused to do it. It was her choice and it was rebellion. She continued to go through the motions of church life but it was empty, because it was not honest. She refused to allow anyone to get close enough to destroy the sandcastle and eventually she faded away into her lonely empty world.

Temptation finds a resting place when our minds entertain it. The way in is the way out. Capturing one thought at a time and replacing it with one truth at a time. Inner healing and deliverance are two sides of the same coin that will bring freedom and peace to the soul and break the power of addiction. Our part is to receive the coin and reap the benefits. We choose death or we choose life. It is our choice, one day at a time and one thought at a time. Choose obedience.

CHAPTER 25

DECEITFULNESS OF RICHES

(Jasmine's story)

The German fairytale *Briar Rose* written by the Grimm Brothers was titled *Sleeping Beauty* when adapted into the movie by Disney Studios. Jasmine watched that movie over and over again as a child. The fairies, witches and magic spells enchanted her. But what mesmerized her most was the scene of the prince awakening the beauty from her sleep with a kiss. The words Sleeping Beauty uttered were etched in her young mind... "Oh, you have come at last! I was waiting for you in my dreams. I have waited so long."

Jasmine's prince was handsome and wealthy promising a life of ease and unending devotion. Whenever her parents argued or her father's harsh word lashed out like a whip, she would wrap herself in her fantasy like a soothing blanket. Her family moved frequently staying one jump ahead of creditors. Her father's drinking and her mother's constant bouts with illness kept them at the threshold of poverty.

When Jasmine was thirteen, she was invited to a youth camp for a week. It was there that she came to hear about the love of God in sending Jesus to make atonement for the sins of the world. She went forward and prayed asking Jesus to forgive her of her sins and to come into her heart. Joy and peace flooded her soul and for the first time in her young life she felt accepted. The next year was filled with a whirlwind of activities as she threw herself wholeheartedly into the youth group and church life. Then the cycle at home reached its familiar conclusion and the family moved to another city. Jasmine was devastated. Grief and anger were her daily bread and drink. She was isolated and drowning in a sea of depression. Her newfound friends were all having sex, drinking and smoking pot. Slowly she drifted into party life and one day without purpose got lost in the next.

After graduation she went to Hawaii with a couple of her friends. It was there that she met her "Prince Charming." He was more than a dozen years older than her and swept her off her feet. Her youth and beauty invigorated him and his affections flooded her thirsty soul. "They lived happily ever after" echoed in her mind as she fantasized that his kiss would awaken her from her teenage stupor. She convinced herself that eventually he would marry her. Returning to the mainland he lavished her with gifts and soon they were living together. For the first six months she was a queen in his court. Then his attention wandered as the queen became one of his lady's in waiting. Her prince was carved deeply in her heart but no longer frequented her bed. She again was isolated and adrift in a sea of depression. He told her it was business that called him away and each time he lied she would lie to herself. Her closets were full but her days were empty. The day she learned that he had married someone else her world crashed in on her. Her dream had now become a nightmare and in the process alcohol her constant companion.

Nothing really changed for her. She still lived in a beautiful apartment and drove an expensive sports car. Her lover came to visit as before but the lie she now chose to embrace was that he would one day leave his wife for her. Between visits her days melted into each other as a slumbering spirit took over her mind and demonic spirits attached to the alcohol started visiting her dreams. Awake or asleep she found no rest. In desperation she came asking for help. She wanted freedom from the vice grip of alcohol and from the tormenting nightmares. Jasmine was twenty-seven when I met her and I was saddened at the vale of dullness the past ten years had placed over her natural beauty. The counsel Holy Spirit gave Jasmine was direct. If she wanted to be free, she needed to build a bridge to Jesus, cross it and then burn the bridge behind her. God was extending mercy to her. He would forgive her of the past and give her a new life.

And what was her reply to this gracious invitation? Her eyes grew wide with shock at such a thought and in a moment her words revealed her true heart as she replied, "I just want to stop drinking not give up everything else." The alcohol was not her problem, although it was destroying her health and tormenting her dreams. Her lover was not the problem, although his lies kept the fantasy alive. The real culprit that held her captive was greed. It was no longer Prince Charming she held in her heart.

It was his moneybag and she was not willing to let go of the purse strings. Fantasy and self-deception had opened the door to a frog that was no prince. He had placed a hook in her jaw but it was Jasmine who now embraced the hook. She had prostituted herself for a lifestyle that would ultimately destroy her.

A real prince was waiting for her on the other side of the bridge. One who would never leave her or forsake her. One who had given up everything for her and would give her treasures that money could not buy. If she could but turn her whole heart toward Jesus the legal right the spirits of alcohol, immorality and torment had to her would be broken and the stronghold of greed destroyed. Unlike her present lover, Jesus would not withhold his heart from her. Whatever her choice, He would never stop loving her but He would not share her heart with anyone or anything else. He came to set her free. What would it profit her to gain the whole world and lose her eternal soul? Could she find the courage to let go of that moneybag? The choice remained hers.

Three years later Jasmine called to say she had finally let go of the moneybag. She had crossed the bridge and burned it. She had returned to the ministry that had first introduced her to Jesus. It was not without a struggle but after two years in a rehab program she was healed and restored to the happy life she had once enjoyed with Jesus as a young teenager.

Is there a bridge you need to build and cross over? Will you light the match to your past and allow Jesus to embrace you and give you a beautiful future? Whatever you have done or failed to do you can leave it all behind. Jesus is the only real Prince Charming who has come to awaken you. Turn to Him with your full heart and call out His name. He will give you a new identity in Him. If you do, you too will awaken to His love and say to Him "Oh, you have come at last! I was waiting for you in my dreams. I have waited so long." The choice remains yours.

"Return, you backsliding children, and I will heal your backsliding" (Jeremiah 3:22a).

CHAPTER 26

REGRET

The windows on one wall in my office are floor to ceiling. Through those windows I can see a park, a walkway, and a horse trail. The windows are covered with reflective film. I can see out but no one can see in. When I arrived to work one morning, I heard an unusual noise. A small bird was furiously fluttering up and down the window. It was pecking and fluttering in an effort to fly into the reflection it saw in the window of the park and the horse trail. The only thing between the window and the park is a small hedge. The bird would occasionally hop onto the hedge and rest. I could hear other birds singing and the little bird would join in the serenade and then turn toward the window and resume its effort to fly toward the image in the glass.

This lovely little bird was trying very hard but going nowhere. It was persistent but it was deceived. Perhaps it was growing stronger through the effort but it was still going nowhere in its frustrated and confused efforts. All the bird had to do was turn around and fly away to enjoy the park. Instead it kept doing the same thing over and over with no results. I tried to help the bird. I tapped on the window but it did not turn around. I thought of taking a broom outside and helping the bird fly away but I had calls coming in and work to get done so I just tried to ignore the struggle.

For over an hour that little bird kept trying to fly toward what it saw in the window. Suddenly the bird turned around and flew away toward the horse trail. I was relieved that it had flown away and amazed at its perseverance. Was it perseverance or lunacy? One definition of insanity is doing the same thing over and over again expecting to get a different result. Throughout the day other birds came but none of them stayed at the task as long as that first little bird.

I had been in this specific office for six years and never before had a bird tried to fly through the window with such determination. I asked the Lord what He was trying to show me. The reply I heard in my spirit was "regret." The dictionary defines regret as feeling sad or disappointed over something that has happened or been done, especially a loss or a missed opportunity.

Many people are like that first persistent bird. They keep looking at the past as if they can relive it and change it. They regret what they did or failed to do, or what was done to them by others, and how that choice or event or their reaction to it changed the course of their lives. Even though Jesus has set them free, they can't enjoy life because they are stuck in the past.

Like the persistent bird, it is madness to keep doing the same thing and think we will get a different result. We can't change what happened or relive the event and make it turn out better.

Refusing to believe in the power of the Blood of Jesus to heal our past is having a form of godliness but denying the power of what He did on Calvary. Jesus bore our past on the cross. We don't have to live with regret. Yet we continue to hold on to it as if it were a medal of honor when really it is a chain of bondage. As long as our focus is on what we regret, we can't move forward. Like the bird, we will be frustrated and confused, wasting valuable time and emotional energy. Jesus does not want us to be focused on what we can never change. He wants us to turn around and move toward the good future He has planned for us.

Each bird had a choice as to how long it continued in futile efforts to fly through the window. It all boils down to choice. How long we are going to keep looking back and regretting what happened, wishing that things had been different. You can't drive forward if you are looking in the rear-view mirror. And the decision to keep looking back will impact your ability to safely progress in life. God promises to heal our broken hearts and bind up our wounds, but He can't do it if we insist on holding on to them.

In a dream I saw myself lying down reading a book. With one hand I was holding the book and with the other I was petting a small black kitten that was on my chest. The kitten was named Regret. I heard the Lord say loudly, "Stop it! Do not make a friend of it or it will choke your life away." We must decide to stop playing with regret in our mind. It won't come easily because our mind has had many years of practice focusing on the past. The way out is to get our eyes off the past and set them on the future.

The winepress called life exposes our flaws, foolishness, self-will and pride. It all brings regret that must be aggressively fought. We can choose to believe that God is a good God who will work all things together for good for those that love Him. Even our regrets can be turned for good if we let go of them and allow God to heal us and use those experiences to help us help others. "Forgetting the things that are behind, we reach for those things which are before, pressing toward the mark for the prize of the high calling of God in Christ Jesus" (Philippians 3:13-14).

Regret is a form of grief. It is part of life on this planet but we don't have to hold on to it. We are not denying the fact that bad things happened but we are denying those things a right to hold us in perpetual grief. We are directed to repent from dead works and regret is a dead work. To repent, on the other hand, is positive. It is admitting our part in what went wrong and turning away from it.

The remedy for all of it is Jesus who can sympathize with our weaknesses. We can choose to wallow in the pain and disappointment or we can choose to be healed. We can decide to keep going back to it, like the little sparrow at the window or we can choose to turn and fly to the new thing that Jesus offers us. He wants us to be known not for what we were but for who we are in Him.

"Remember not the former things, neither think on the things of the past. Behold, I will do a new thing: now it shall spring forth, shall you not know it? I will even make a way in the wilderness and rivers in the desert" (Isaiah 43:18,19).

CHAPTER 27

WHAT TIME IS IT?

Jesus knew when it was time to turn the tables because people had made His Father's house a house of merchandise instead of a house of prayer. He also knew when it was time to keep His mouth shut and turn the other cheek allowing Himself to be tortured and killed so that we could have salvation and abundant life. He knew what to do and when to do it because of His intimate relationship with the Father. Out of that relationship flowed the wisdom to know if it was time to turn the tables or turn the other cheek. Could Jesus have healed the blind man one day earlier or one day later? No, because He only said and did what the Father told Him and showed Him. Jesus healed the blind man on the right day, at the right time and in the right way.

At one point Moses and all the people ascended unto the hill of the Lord. When they came down Joshua chose to stay in the presence of Lord. He chose to not only ascend but to abide and it brought him much favor. It is in abiding that we will enter into that intimate relationship with the Father.

When the people of Israel asked for water in the desert Moses struck the rock as the Lord directed him and water came forth. Forty years later when again the people asked for water God told Moses to stand and speak to the rock. He spoke in anger to the people and then struck the rock. Moses lost his reward of entering into the Promised Land because he could not transition to do the new thing and dishonored God. Saul did the right thing at the wrong time. He was directed to wait for the prophet who would offer a sacrifice unto the Lord. He got impatient waiting for the prophet to arrive and decided to burn the sacrifice himself. It cost him his kingdom.

Jesus said that from the days of John the Baptist until now the kingdom suffers violence and the violent take it by force. He also said whoever does not receive as a child cannot enter the kingdom of God (Matthew 11:12 and Mark 10:15). You can't be taking the kingdom by force and be receiving the kingdom as a child without force at the same time. We are called to do both. So, the question is what time is it? Is it time to be a warrior or time to be a child?

As believers we must learn the value of asking, seeking and waiting on the Lord. Is it time to sell or to buy? Is it time to take a job or leave a job, to speak up or to hold your tongue? Most of us miss it in the timing by either running ahead of God or lagging behind. But we want to be people who are in step with the Lord.

It is always time to be humble, to forgive, to love and trust God. But things that are not absolutes are why we need the Holy Spirit to help and direct us. It is a good thing to teach others but when someone is drowning is not the time to teach someone to swim. We must use wisdom. Ask for ears to hear, eyes to see and a heart to understand what the Spirit of God is saying and wisdom of how and when to do it.

In order to see and hear correctly we must be in agreement with God and that agreement comes through knowledge of the Word, knowledge about the character of God and discernment of what the Holy Spirit is saying. As with Jesus, it is born out of intimate relationship with the Father. There is no other way to receive it. There is no other way to know if it is a turn the table moment or a turn the other cheek moment. Ask the Lord for the anointing of the sons of Issachar who had the ability to know the times and the seasons. Ask for the gift of discernment.

I had taken a new job and was busy putting systems in place and getting thing in order. The doctor who owned the practice was a proud and handsome man, married with a young daughter. It had been three months and I was being praised for the positive changes and the progress of organizing his office. However, I had an uneasy feeling whenever I was in the office. At first, I thought it was the normal jitters of starting a new job and adjusting to the environment. However, I started to realize that I only experienced that uneasy feeling when the doctor was around. Something was off with him but I could not pin point the problem, so I began to pray.

A month later the doctor told me there were administrative matters that needed attention and asked me to come in on Saturday morning to discuss them. I agreed but something in my spirit felt uncomfortable. Although I had only been there a few months I realized something was wrong. It was well concealed but not from the Holy Spirit. By praying in the Spirit, I became aware that women who would report to him that their husbands were not satisfied with their sex life were scheduled to meet with the doctor after normal office hours. The word that kept showing up in charts was "mentor." Which he did in the adjacent bedroom suite. When he asked me to meet with him the Holy Spirit warned me not to go alone.

I called my sister and asked her to go with me to the appointment and wait in the lobby while we had our meeting. That uncomfortable feeling was a prompting of the Holy Spirit although I did not know it at the time. When we arrived on Saturday the doctor was visibly upset that I had brought someone with me. The meeting was brief and shallow. At that point he could have just walked away. Instead he bluntly told me that in order for me to keep my job I had to sleep with him. To which I responded that I would do no such thing. Instead he was going to lay me off and pay my medical insurance for three months. He laughed at my response and asked what made me think he would do that. To which I responded that if he did not, I would report the sex clinic he had going on adjacent to his office. His jaw dropped and he conceded wanting to have no further discussion. The following Monday I received my layoff notice which gave me some unemployment income while I looked for another job and my medical insurance was paid for the next three months.

When I confronted him, I was saying what the Holy Spirit had told me not because I had hard evidence but because I trusted the Holy Spirit. The look on his face told me I was right. This was a turn the table moment. Praying in the Spirit helped me and the Holy Spirit got me out of that horrible situation.

Fast forward a few years and I am now working for a very successful general contractor. The housing market was booming and the owner decided to diversify. He opened a jet ski business and a quarter horse breeding venture. All three businesses were doing well for a few years. Slowly the housing market changed and his accountant advised him to close the jet-ski and quarter horse ventures because the construction company would not be able to sustain all three businesses as the market changed. He did not listen and ended up losing all three businesses. All the employees were told to look for other work as he was facing bankruptcy.

I asked the Holy Spirit for direction and began to pray in the Spirit. Two days after the bankruptcy news I was listening to a teaching on the parable of the good Samaritan. The Holy Spirit prompted me through that message to help this man. On Monday morning I told him that instead of looking for another job I would stay and help him close things out. I spent six weeks making calls, sending letters, responding to employment verifications and packing boxes. I stayed until the furniture was carried out the door. He was very grateful for the help and I was trusting God to take care of me. One week after the office officially closed, I got a call from the wife of one of my former co-workers who offered me a job with no interview and no delay. The Lord had looked ahead and made provision for me. It was a turn the other cheek moment.

Five months later I had a call from the contractor's wife who told me that the angels were singing in heaven because her husband had received Jesus as his Savior and Lord. The financial test and trial had brought him to his knees and in his brokenness, he had reached out to God. Eventually he opened another jet ski business that prospered.

A friend knows the heart of a friend. Through years of going through life together they become intimately acquainted with each other. Trust joins them and agreement keeps them bound. Agreement with God binds us to His will and purposes. We can know His heart by spending quality time with Him. By reading the scriptures we renew our minds and come to know His character. The Lord speaks to us spirit to spirit. The Holy Spirit is our internal G.P.S. He will tell us if it is time to be a child and trust Him or time to be a warrior and take the land. Praying in tongues quiets the mind and allows us to be sensitive in our spirits in order to discern what to do and when to do it or what not to do and what not to say. Allow the Holy Spirit to have His way, thank Him for the mysteries you are praying in the Spirit and receive the answer to those prayers by faith. You too can know what time it is.

Is it time for you to discover who He created you to be? It is time to be courageous and break ungodly soul ties and uproot judgments, anger and offenses? Is it time to dismantle the sandcastles and cemented thinking? Is it time to be free of greed, self-pity, regret, disappointment and emotional brokenness? Is it time to take off the handcuffs of self-condemnation? You get to choose how much of Jesus you want. Restoration is His desire for you. Take the step and cross the threshold out of darkness and into His glorious light. The Heavenly Father wants you to come out of the shadows and will run to help you. The choice is yours. Choose life!

CHAPTER 28

PRAYER OF DEDICATION AND RESTORATION

John 3:16 tells us that God so loved the world, that he gave His only begotten Son, that whosoever would believe in Him should not perish, but have everlasting life. Jesus died on the cross and went to hell for one reason: to pay the price for sin which keeps man from relationship with the Heavenly Father. Anyone who will choose to believe in Jesus will be restore to their position as a child of God. This choice is one made of our free will.

If you make this choice, you will experience a spiritual re-birth and take on the nature of God. Your spirit will then be sealed by the Holy Spirits (restoration of your human spirit). From that point forward the restoration of your soul will begin (John 3: 3-7.)

If you are ready to choose Jesus and be born again pray these words from the depths of your heart.

Heavenly Father I thank you for loving me and sending Jesus to die on the cross for me. I believe that Jesus was punished and paid the price I owed so that I could be forgiven and come into relationship with you. Holy Spirit thank you for raising Jesus from the dead so that I could be born again and receive eternal life.

Heavenly Father, I acknowledge that You desire every area of my life to be restored and brought into divine order. I acknowledge that Jesus has paid the price for that restoration by the shedding of His blood. Please restore every good thing in my life that has been stolen. Jesus came to destroy the works of the evil one. I set myself in agreement with Jesus and all that He has done and all that the Holy Spirit is doing for me and in me now that I am Your child.

Thank You Father, for assigning specific spiritual authority over me. Jesus as my Good Shepherd, High Priest and Deliverer and the Holy Spirit as my Teacher, Comforter and Guide. Thank You for the holy angels that you have assigned to help me and who fight on my behalf. Thank You for the ministers (evangelist, pastors, teachers and prophets) that You have appointed to help carry out the work of the rebuilding of my life.

Holy Spirit please release grace to those assigned to build and prosper my life. I do not receive any words spoken over me or about me that are not from You but I bless and receive the words which are from You. I yield to Your work to take away the trash from my life and rebuild my walls.

Lord Jesus I acknowledge that I have been created by You and ask You to reveal yourself to me. You determined before the foundations of the world that I should be in a specific location, at a specific time in history and for a specific call and purpose. I yield to that call upon my life and will not accept any other plan.

I put the Blood of Jesus, the fire of God, the work of the cross and the power of the Holy Spirit between my life and all demonic spirits. I bind every spirit of jealousy and hatred and command them to go from me now. I bring the Blood of Jesus against every mocking spirit and every spirit of ridicule, scoffing and contempt. In the name of Jesus, I take authority over every spirit of anger, fury, insult and retaliation. I break the power of all demonic plots and intimidation. I ask Your holy angels to destroy all evil altars built against my life and all generational strongholds. I come out of agreement and break any evil covenants that I, or my ancestors, have made.

Holy Spirit I ask You to bring divine order to my thoughts and break the power of every spirit that would keep me from full restoration. I acknowledge that You are the maker of heaven and earth and the Author and Finisher of my faith. I thank You for Your faithfulness in completing that which You have begun in my life. Amen

The right, privilege, and power to decide has been left in your hands. Choose to decree and declare what the Word of God says about who you are and what you can do. Use the Word of God to silence the enemy just as Jesus did when He was tempted in the wilderness. (see Luke 4:1-13).

PRAYER OF DECLARATION

I choose to bow my knees unto the Father of our Lord Jesus Christ. (Ephesians 3:14)

I embrace the truth that I am a child of God by faith in Jesus Christ. (Galatians 3:26)

I accept God's forgiveness and love. (Ephesians 1:4-7)

I receive the grace of God for my life. (2 Corinthians 12:9a)

I receive the spirit of wisdom and revelation in the knowledge of Christ. (Ephesians 1:17)

I receive the strength of the Holy Spirit in my inner man. (Ephesians 3:14)

I believe that God is faithful. (1 Corinthians 1:9)

I choose not to judge or condemn but rather to forgive as I have been forgiven. (Luke 6:37)

I choose to allow the Heavenly Father to comfort me. (1 Corinthians 1:4)

I choose to dwell in the secret place of the most High (Jesus) and abide under the shadow of the Almighty (Holy Spirit). (Psalm 91:1)

I choose to hope, believing that what He promised He is able to perform. (Romans 4:21)

I will not to condemn myself because I am in Christ Jesus. I choose to walk after the Spirit and not after the flesh. (Romans 8:1)

I choose the law of the Spirit of life in Christ Jesus which has made me free from the law of sin and death. (Romans 8:2)

I break any judgments I have made against others and against my-self. (Matthew 7:12)

I renounce any unholy vows I have made and any lies I have be-lieved. (Ephesians 4:17-24)

I cast my cares upon the Lord because He cares for me. (1Peter 5:7)

I will obey God rather than man. (Acts 5:29)

I put away from me all bitterness, wrath, anger, clamor, evil speak-ing, and malice. I choose to be kind, tender hearted, forgiving others, even as God has forgiven me. (Ephesians 4: 31-32)

I choose not to be deceived by vain and empty words. (Ephesians 5:6)

I choose to be strong in the Lord and in the power of His might. (Ephesians 6:10)

I am a child of obedience. (James 1:22 and 1 Samuel 15:22-23)

I will know the truth and the truth will set me free. (John 8:32)

I choose not to be afraid, because the Lord is with me. His word and His Spirit comfort me. (Psalms 23:4)

I will let patience have its perfect work, that I may be whole and entire lacking nothing. (James 1:4)

I reject fear and I choose to accepts the spirit of power, love and sound mind. (2 Timothy 1:7)

I choose not to be overcome by evil, but to overcome evil with good. (Romans 12:21)

I believe that I can do all things through Christ who strengthens me. (Philippians 4:13)

I thank God who supplies all my needs according to His riches in glory by Christ Jesus. (Philippians 4:19)

I put my trust in God. I will not be afraid of what man can do to me. (Psalm 56:11)

I receive the peace Jesus said He has given me. I will not to let my heart be troubled or be afraid. (John 14:27)

I receive the help the Lord God has for me. I will not be confounded. I choose to set my face like a flint, and I know that I shall not be ashamed. (Isaiah 50:7)

I will not be anxious for anything; but in everything by prayer and supplication with thanksgiving I let my requests be made known unto God. I receive the peace of God, which passes all understanding and it shall keep my heart and mind through Christ Jesus. (Philippians 4:6,7)

I believe and am persuaded, that neither death, nor life, no angels, no principalities, nor powers, nor things present, not things to come, nor height, nor depth nor any other creature, shall be able to separate me from the love of God which is in Christ Jesus my Lord. (Romans 8:38, 39)

I choose to wait on the Lord and to be of good courage, and He will strengthen my heart. (Psalm 27:14)

ABOUT THE AUTHOR

Carmen Esther Sandoval is an administrative professional with over 30 years of experience in Administrative Management and Human Resources. She has supported top management of both large and small organizations.

Carmen committed her life to the Lord Jesus Christ in 1977. Having experienced many physical and emotional healings and miracles for herself and in the lives of others her passion is to see people come to know who they are in Christ and what He can do for them and through them by the power of the Holy Spirit.

Carmen was ordained a Minister of the Gospel in 2002 at New Creation Outreach in Anaheim, and again in 2014 at Reign Christian Fellowship in San Juan Capistrano. She trained under Dr. Norvel Hayes, Pastor John Wimber, Pastor Mario Procopio and Pastor Charles Colletti..

She has served for over twenty years through personal prayer ministry, building up the Body of Christ one person at a time. Carmen was part of the Small Team Ministry at the Anaheim Vineyard, leader of the Mobile Prayer Team at the Laguna Niguel Vineyard, and a member of the Fathers Touch Ministry in Mission Viejo. For the past five years Carmen has served as Director of the Healing Rooms of Orange County in San Juan Capistrano. The Healing Rooms is an outreach ministry associated with the International Association of Healing Rooms, in Spokane, Washington (IAHR).

While Jesus was on the earth He healed the sick, cast out demons and performed miracles. Carmen believes Jesus is doing the same today and will use humble and yielded sons and daughters of God to manifest His great love to the world.

Carmen can be reached at: carmen@upwordfocuspro.com.

Please visit her website at www.upwardfocuspro.com